DESIGNS of DESIRE

TEMPESTE O'RILEY

Dreamspinner Press

Published by
Dreamspinner Press
5032 Capital Circle SW
Ste 2, PMB# 279
Tallahassee, FL 32305-7886
USA
http://www.dreamspinnerpress.com/

Cover Art by Reese Dante
http://www.reesedante.com

Cover content is being used for illustrative purposes only
and any person depicted on the cover is a model.

ISBN: 978-1-62798-004-3
Digital ISBN: 978-1-62798-005-0

Printed in the United States of America
First Edition
July 2013

For the Mels, Dianne, Andrew, and Nikki; thanks for encouraging and kicking me in the pants when needed. And for my personal hero, Markus; thank you for being you!

I'm so proud to know you all.

To everyone that has ever felt betrayed by both others and their own bodies, never give up hope because your HEA is out there waiting for you! Love has no limits....

chapter one

667, 668, 669....

A file slapped the desk in front of James, distracting him from his attempt at counting the dots in the ceiling tiles above him.

"I *know* you're busy and all," Brian said, his usual sneer in place. "But do you think you'll have time to help a new client?" The man just lived to give him a hard time.

James took a deep breath. He desperately hoped his hatred of the man towering over him didn't show. James knew open displays of boredom pissed Brian off, but James hadn't had a prospective or existing client call in two days. He'd finished his purchasing reports, sent the work orders and e-mail. All calls done. What else was he supposed to do?

"Sure, Brian. Let me see what we've got, and I'll head right out," James replied. He tried to sound upbeat. It wasn't that he didn't like his job; he did. But Brian hated him, and he always got the leftovers—usually clients the other designers did not want for one reason or another.

"I'm sure this one's right up your—" Cough. "—alley," Brian finished with a snicker.

James never figured out how someone so hateful and narrow-minded as Brian stood working in their field, much less kept his job. In James's opinion, art, even corporate branding and design, should attract people with a bit more open-mindedness. He had a few ideas on the latter but kept his opinions, and gutter-mind, to himself.

Forcing a smile across his face as he opened the folder in front of him, James called out to Brian's retreating form, "No worries, boss."

Brian paused and turned to look over his shoulder and with a nasty smile added, "Oh, and the guy'll be here in about ten minutes. Don't screw up."

Ten minutes? Seriously?

He started to peruse the new client information, pleased that at least the file seemed to be complete—charts, images, budget, etc.— and his phone rang. He answered on the second ring. "Good morning, James Bryant speaking."

"Ah, Jamie, got the file yet? 'Cuz let me tell you, this one's something else" came the disembodied voice of his best friend and co-worker, Chase Manning. "He's not like most of the scraps Brian-the-dick tosses you."

"I'm sure I can handle whatever he sends my way. The clients aren't usually as difficult as Brian and the others make them seem. They just don't want to deal with high maintenance or quirky. Which, when you consider the job, makes no sense. But—"

"Jamie, dear," Chase said, cutting him off. "That's not it at all. This guy's hot, and I mean H-O-T, hot. He's waiting for you already and man, I so wish I had your job today," he practically squealed. "So hurry up and get your sexy ass down here. Now."

"Shh.... Don't be so loud. The last thing I need is you to offend a new client. Now, go back to work and let me read over the file, would ya?" He shook his head and clicked off his Bluetooth. James glanced over the information for his new client. *Seth Burns?* Carl, their senior manager, had been trying to get Mr. Burns of Carrington Enterprises as a client for years. *Wonder what he's looking for and how this project slipped past Brian to me?*

Setting it aside, James pulled out his messenger bag and loaded it with the folder. He already had all his staples in there: pens, pencils, a notebook or two, and a couple of sketch pads. He carefully hung it across his neck and shoulder so the bag wouldn't slip. He preferred his backpack, but his *boss* frowned on "casual."

James gathered his forearm crutches, the plain black ones he only used for work, and he began the arduous task of getting up before he slipped his arms through the cuffs.

Once satisfied he wasn't forgetting anything, James slung himself down the hall to the elevator, where he waited. He hated standing there, given Brian's office faced the hall.

When James reached the main floor, Chase seemed to vibrate as he waited for him. His face reminded James of a child at Disney World instead of the twenty-five-year-old man he actually was.

"Do you want to meet with him down here in one of the conference rooms?" Chase pleaded, batting his eyes for full effect. He knew better than to act like that, but, *oh well.*

"Relax, Chase," James said with a smile. Chase, his sometimes assistant and best friend, always worried about James walking too much, but then he never managed to understand the idea of limitations versus inability. James could walk, though he couldn't walk far or carry much of anything. He simply needed his crutches. Limitations James loathed but had learned to accept.

"I just hate you traipsing up and down the halls. I wish—"

"Don't," James snapped harder than he'd meant to. "Sorry. You know I appreciate your concern, but I'm a big boy and can manage fine. Now, go back to your desk and do your job so I can do mine."

With a huff, Chase flounced back to his desk. "Fine," he called over his shoulder. "Be that way."

James ignored him and pushed on, maneuvering himself around to reception to meet his new client.

He looked around and nearly gasped. The only man sitting in the waiting area was... beautiful. There was no other way to describe him. Dark hair, a straight, aristocratic nose, and a full, pouty bottom lip. And built? He wasn't bulky but smooth and toned. The kind of body that comes from serious work and forethought.

Yummy, James thought but quickly corrected his wayward mind. *He's here for my work services, not me.* At twenty-eight, he had already given up on finding his prince. He didn't even bother trying anymore. He knew he was a good-looking man—having been told so many times over the years—but Victor, his ex, had taught him that he was too much trouble for a real relationship. Not like anyone asked him out since the *accident* and the stupid sticks, anyways. *Focus on the job!*

The man rose and held out his hand. "Mr. Bryant, I presume."

"Yes, and you're Seth Burns, correct?" James replied, pausing in his motions to take the crutch from his right hand and offer it in return for the handshake.

Seth nodded, a bright smile stretched across his perfect face.

"Wonderful," James said. "I apologize for the wait. Now, if you would come with me. I'd like to discuss what you're looking for, and what I can do for you." James readjusted his crutches, turned, and headed toward the conference room he used on the first floor.

As they approached the door, James grabbed for the handle. *Humph.* Seth beat him to it, pushing the door open. Once the initial surprise died, he was left wondering why Mr. Burns had done that— no one but Chase helped him at the office. The only other time anyone helped was out of pity. He hated pity.

"Um, thanks," he mumbled, trying to sound grateful instead of mildly annoyed.

"You seemed to have your hands full and mine weren't," Seth said with a shrug.

James knew his hands were full, but they always were. He hated being viewed as less of a man, or a cripple, because of the sticks he used to help him walk.

"Right, thank you," he said, sliding into one of the rolling leather chairs at the back of the long cherrywood table. He placed his crutches against the closest wall for easy retrieval.

James gestured to the chair across the conference table and hoped Seth would sit. He hated to be stood over. Seth smiled and settled into the chair indicated. "Now, what can I do for you, sir?"

"We, Carrington Enterprises, are beginning a new venture and hope you can help with designs. Companies I can manage; design and draw, not so much."

James nodded at Seth's pause.

"Let me start by explaining the project you will brand. We're opening a new hotel chain. This will be a little different than your usual hotel, though. Each site will be more like a large bed and breakfast, but they will cater to the GLBT community. It's often an issue when a couple wants to vacation. They have to consider the area, the hotel, the other patrons even if they want to do something as simple as hold hands. That is, if they don't want to be met with hate or possible violence."

James wasn't sure which impressed him more, the wonderful idea behind the hotel or the deep, commanding voice that instilled confidence in everything Seth said.

Obviously unaware of James's internal dialog, Seth continued his spiel. "With our liberal policies and views, we have decided to make a place where judgment doesn't exist. At least, that's the theory."

God, that voice! James shivered.

"Also, each site will have a club, bar, or restaurant attached. So, this will be an ongoing project, not a one-shot deal." When finished with his little speech, Seth seemed inordinately pleased with the idea.

No wonder Brian gave me the account. He didn't realize he had spoken aloud until Seth glowered at him.

"Excuse me?" Seth snapped. "I was assured you have no personal issues or biases that might hinder your ability to provide the needed work. Was I incorrectly informed?"

"No. No, sir. I apologize for my comment. It was out of line," James said in a rush, trying to smooth over the obvious irritation his thoughtless words had caused.

"Are you able to do the branding or should I continue elsewhere?" Seth demanded.

"You misunderstand, Mr. Burns. I had wondered why I was given your account, considering I'm not one of the senior designers and your account would normally be reserved for one of them. Now that I hear what the project is, I understand why I was chosen." He knew he was babbling but he couldn't help it. "You see, I'm the only openly gay designer here and my family runs a small bed and breakfast. This project is perfect. In fact, once we have the branding set up, I'm sure I can point you in the right direction for some specialized marketing. Magazines, newspapers, websites, et cetera. We will help you with all of that, as well." James tried to restrain the extent of his excitement over the project, but was unsure how successful he was. He didn't want to seem flippant or inexperienced after admitting he was a junior designer with Skye Designs.

Seth raised an eyebrow and smiled. "Excited, are we? Carl said you were the man for the job. I guess he was right if enthusiasm counts. I have a full write-up of what we need and what we do and do not want to incorporate into the brand." His smile fell and he became all business again. "This is an upscale getaway, not a high-priced bathhouse."

"Understood, sir. I think the idea will work in areas with a large enough population of GLBT and open-minded people." His hands itched to begin sketching and planning.

"Good. Once you've read over everything and start your designing, I want you to visit the site we chose for the first hotel. It's here in Milwaukee, so it shouldn't be too far for you. Would you be ready by Friday?" At James's accord, Seth opened his briefcase and began pulling out folders and large manila envelopes and setting them in front of James. He paused, peered up at James, and blinked hard. "I should call someone to carry these things for you," he mumbled, glancing at the items and toward James's crutches. "You can't fit all this in your bag."

James pinched the bridge of his nose while counting to ten in his head. *Why do they always see the sticks instead of me?* "Mr. Burns."

"Seth, please," he interrupted, giving James a soft smile.

"Seth, Chase acts as my assistant when needed. He will tend to anything I can't transfer up to my office personally. There is no need to be concerned."

A strange look flashed across Seth's face, but his expression quickly returned to his previous in-command smile. "Very good then."

They chatted a bit about ideas and plans before Seth shifted his coat sleeve back to check his watch. With a slight frown, he said, "Well, I need to head back to the office. I will leave this all in your fine hands, James. Please call me here." He pulled out his business card and wrote something on the back. "I look forward to our next meeting."

Seth held out his hand. James flexed his fingers and clasped the offering. He knew this was for work, but somehow it felt different this time. Warm and strong, the grip shot tingles up his arm. Seth seemed to hold on a little longer than necessary for business needs. It had been so long since a man touched him, at least without violence or pain. James shook off the thought he might be interested. Beautiful men like Seth didn't waste their time on guys like him. Besides, he wasn't certain he wanted to go down such a painful road again.

James stood in the doorway, watching Seth saunter out the main doors, wishing for something, though not really sure what.

"So," Chase said, bounding into the room. "Is he hot, or is he *hot*?"

"Hot? Yes. But, he's also my new client and I'm not positive he's gay. Even if he is, he's probably taken. Men like him don't stay single for long. Anyways, help me get all this upstairs. I need to get started. He wants me to visit the local site this Friday."

DRIVING through the morning fog, James headed to the hotel construction site. Seth had assured him it was almost completed and was safe to visit. James pulled in and parked up front, then grabbed his backpack—the one he used outside the office to carry items—off the passenger seat. James slung the pack onto his back. He set his sticks in the gravel of the parking area, climbed out of his blue CRV, and headed up the wide, stonework stairs to the main entrance of the soon-to-be hotel. *Hate stairs*, he sulked. The ramp wasn't finished yet.

Once he entered the foyer, James allowed his gaze to wander around the entryway, taking in the welcoming setting. Noticing a worker passing through, he asked, "Excuse me. Do you know where I can find Mr. Burns?"

"Yeah, he's in the manager's office over there." The man was covered in dust. He gestured toward a closed door near a large desk, then continued on his way. James couldn't help looking around once more to admire the rich wood tones, marble tiled floors, and beautiful crown molding, before he headed off in the right direction.

Before he could knock, the door swung open and a harried-looking woman stormed out, slamming it so hard it popped back open. *Maybe now isn't the best time*, he thought and started to turn away when Mr. Burns appeared in the doorway.

"James," he said. "Thank God you're here. Please tell me you brought some ideas, before Stacey drives me to drink. She wants to start painting but can't until we have everything settled with the designs."

The way Seth's eyes pierced him made James feel both nervous and ten feet tall at the same time. "If you have some place I can set up, sure. I have a few designs for you to look over." He kept wondering why they had waited so long to employ Skye Designs. *Normally you do all the branding much earlier in the project.*

Motioning down the hallway, Seth led him into a large room—probably meant to be a conference or reception room, considering the carpet and acoustic tiles in the ceiling. "Come in. What can I do to help?" he asked, watching James settle into a comfortable chair before unloading his pack.

James was nervous. He'd never had such a significant or large account before, but he was excited as well. "We normally have the designs approved before getting to this point, but I'll do my best to catch up. Give me just a minute to set up, then you can see what I have."

"We'll get to that in a few. I want you to finish setting up then come with me."

James stopped midmotion and looked up, confused. "I thought—" He shook his head. "Never mind. Okay."

Seth led James out of the room, into a wide hallway with large windows spilling filtered sunlight onto the veined marble floor, and began showing him around. Seth stayed close, so close James occasionally caught a whiff of his intoxicating scent, something bright yet deep—cardamom and cedar with a light musk. He wasn't sure, but he was beginning to think just being near Seth could become a delicious addiction.

As they exited the elevator on the second floor, James stopped dead in his tracks. His heart beat so fast and loud he felt certain Seth would hear it slamming into his ribs. He stared ahead and prayed he was having a terrible nightmare. Those he could wake up from. *Please!*

Standing there, looking him up and down, was a phantom from his past. Victor d'Leone was even more powerfully built than the last time he had seen him. He stood in the hall, his arms crossed over his barrel chest, scowling. The sea-foam green eyes James once thought so beautiful and loving now bored holes through him. The ghosts of the last time Vic had been near him shot pain-filled shards of memory through him. *Away.* Yes, he had to get away.

"I... I... I...," James stammered. He scrambled back into the elevator and almost fell when his left crutch slipped on the metal edging. He punched the close door button repeatedly while fighting the panic attack threatening to destroy his job and sanity. "No, no, no. Not happening," he mumbled.

He hadn't waited for Seth to react, nor had he explained anything; he'd just bolted. James headed toward the exit as soon as the elevator doors opened—*forget the damn presentation.* He scrambled for the steps, desperate to reach the car before he completely lost it.

Life was never that easy.

Seth appeared out of nowhere, sprinting after him in his expensive Armani suit and custom leather shoes. "James! Stop!" he commanded.

Fighting the panic, James tried to get a hold of himself. *Stop? Is he nuts?* "I can't be here. I—I'll come back later." *With protection!*

A powerful hand grasped his right arm. Startled, he stopped. Staring at the hand that bound him to his worst nightmare, he begged, "Please, let me go."

Try as he might, he couldn't stop the panic and fear as it suffocated him.

chapter two

"JAMES," Seth said, placing his other hand on James's lower back. Exerting gentle pressure, he steered James away from the front doors, toward the office. He was desperate to leave, but couldn't bring himself to pull away from the warmth and strength of Seth's hands.

"Take a deep breath." Seth's soft command offered shelter. He found himself doing just that as Seth guided him into a chair. Seth took his crutches from him and leaned them against the desk.

James struggled to calm down and not do anything else to embarrass himself. His gaze flicked repeatedly to the door, as he was afraid Victor might follow like Seth had. In his mind he knew he was safe, but he'd be damned if the rest of him wanted to listen.

Seth placed a cold bottle of water in James's hand, giving him something to clutch other than his own fingers. "Drink, slowly," he instructed.

Without thinking, he followed Seth's directions, grateful for the sanctuary and care. He wasn't sure why, but Seth's take-control way of handling him soothed his frayed psyche in a way he hadn't expected—and wasn't sure he wanted to like.

Seth didn't say anything for a long time. He just continued to keep physical contact with James, his hand on his shoulder. He didn't exert pressure or move in any way but left it there for comfort and support.

"Feel better?" Seth asked once James's breathing had returned to almost normal.

With a nod, James replied, "Yes. Sorry about that. Um, is he— why is he here?" James knew it was probably a stupid question, but he didn't care. Moving away from that warm, strong hand would hurt too, though.

"Vic? I don't know what your problem is with each other, but he's the assistant foreman for the construction crew working here. He's an ass, but I've never seen him look like that, nor have I seen anyone react to him as you did." He waited but didn't ask why James had panicked, although James was sure he was dying to.

"I need to get my things and leave, Mr. Burns. If this is his workplace then it's me that needs to go. I will be happy to meet you at your office or mine, if you'd rather. I apologize for my behavior and hope you won't hold it against me or Skye Designs," James said. He sat up straight and tried to regain at least a little of his lost dignity.

"I will agree, for now, with moving this to my office. Are you up for an afternoon meeting and presentation?" Seth inquired.

"Yes, sir," James said, sounding a bit more calm and like his usual self.

"I expect to see you at three o'clock sharp." They spoke for a few more minutes, until he was able to convince Seth it was safe to allow him to drive. Seth returned his crutches and walked him to his car, then insisted he would have one of his people transfer the presentation materials to his office for their meeting. Seth only stepped away from James as James settled into his car.

After a quick call to Chase to let him know he'd be out of the office the rest of the day, James went home, lay down on the couch, curled his knees up to his chest, and tried to get through the rest of his panic and pain. He hadn't seen Victor since the cops removed him from James's old apartment, two years ago, having gone so far as to change many of the places he frequented in the hopes of never seeing the man again. And now? Now he may have lost the best account he'd ever had because of that damn man.

WATCHING James panic and run had been painful for Seth. The handsome man had captivated him from the moment their eyes met. His piercing blue orbs and serious demeanor were what he saw first, but once they got to talking, James's enthusiasm and eccentric way of moving his hands while talking—almost like he was sketching his thoughts in the air—made Seth ache to know more about the man, not just his job. But, he couldn't shake the image of James as he trembled on the edge of a full-blown panic attack. *What the hell happened to him?*

"Mel," Seth said after tapping his Bluetooth.

"Yes," he confirmed when the digital voice asked for verification, and moments later he heard his best friend and lawyer on the other end of the line.

"Hey, Seth. What's up?" Mel asked.

"I need you to do me a favor, and I need it fast," Seth said, ignoring basic formalities. *This is Mel, he'll understand.*

"Well, hi to you too. I take it something happened with your new project?"

"More like to my design specialist. I was there but still don't have a damn clue what the hell happened." Seth needed answers and wanted them before his afternoon meeting with James.

"It's a good thing I like you so much, because right now, you're being strange, even for you. What happened? And give me the guy's name; I'll see what I can find."

Seth gave Mel a quick recap and clicked off once Mel promised to send anything he found straight to his phone. He figured he should get some use out of the smartphone he had, and this was the perfect opportunity.

WALKING into the corporate offices of Carrington Enterprises, James looked around and tried to get a feel for the people and the company. While he knew *of* C.E., he'd never been there, and thanks to the morning's disaster, he was nervous.

After he spoke with the receptionist, he sat and waited. The young woman gave him an odd look, though he wasn't sure if it was because of his crutches or something else—since he wasn't at the office and this was a GLBT project, he'd decided to use the rainbow hued set Chase had bought him for his last birthday. Deciding to ignore her, he pulled out one of his sketchbooks and proceeded to tease out alternative designs for his current project and, well, for anything his muse threw his way.

The off-white sheet in front of him faded as shapes and ideas filled his vision. The world receded around him as his muse guided his hand, his heart racing with the thrill of a new creation.

He was deep in his sketching place, that mental realm he always went when inspiration took over, when he became aware someone was watching him. The thought ran through the back of his mind that he should probably find out what the person wanted, but he needed to finish the rough draft first.

He put his pencil down, and the world came back into proper focus. When it did, he realized the person who watched him was not, in fact, the receptionist, but rather Seth Burns, the man he was here to see. The man he'd lost it in front of and now ignored. *Way to win friends and influence, huh.*

"I'm sorry, Mr. Burns," James said. The heat of a blush raced up his throat.

Seth gave him an amused smile. "Come on up, James. We can discuss your presentation as well as your artwork there," he said with a nod toward the pad.

James put the sketchpad away and got to his feet, slowly working his way toward the elevator Seth indicated. "I'm glad you could make it back today," Seth continued and pushed the button for the top floor. "I have a few people upstairs that wish to see your presentation as well. I had all your equipment and papers transferred to my office, though I didn't understand the bits I looked at. I am hoping you can make it more people-friendly. I have to say though,

Stacy, the woman you saw this morning, is in love with one of the packets."

Confused, James wondered which design set she'd looked over. He'd only brought a few of the physical designs, having kept the rest on his laptop for the presentation. "I'll do my best," he mumbled. He caught himself fidgeting and tense again, a state he hated but couldn't do anything about—not with Seth around, anyway.

Once they reached the executive floor and exited, Seth led him to a solid oak door. As they walked in, without knocking, they were met by a handful of others in expensive suits and long faces. It was obvious they were not amused to have been dragged in for this late Friday meeting. Well, five long faces and an excited one that seemed to be going through his things.

"Excuse me, ma'am, but until I have a chance to do the presentation, could you please refrain from rearranging and touching things?" He didn't mean to be snippy, but he hated when people messed with his work before he was ready. *Shouldn't have left the stuff at the site*, he thought, but he'd been in no state to collect and transfer everything himself.

"Stacy, put James's work down. Now," Seth said in such an even voice that the steel behind it was almost hidden.

"Sorry, Seth, but have you seen any of his designs yet?" she asked, her voice high and eyes bright. She returned all of James's things to the desk.

"No, I have not. Now, sit and let the man do his job."

"Yes, sir," she replied, almost meekly. Her demeanor was a far cry from what it had been when she'd stormed out of the hotel manager's office.

Seth sat with the others, looking expectant but calm.

After he rearranged and added a few things, James set about showing the designs he had brought. He offered three options for the hotel plus a few unfinished but excellent design sketches for the restaurant. Each incorporated at least one common GLBT theme, but in a tasteful and subdued way that gave off the class and polish they had asked for while still showing off the sexuality theme the project was tailored around.

They listened and asked questions, but James found Seth's quiet attention unnerving. It also served to keep him aware of every move, shift, or sound the man made, increasing his interest and nervousness—no man had affected James in years, and he was at a loss as to why now, and why this man. Seth looked over the designs; he seemed to see more than the images in front of him, and waited while the others talked, argued, and finally left.

Once they were alone again, Seth looked up, calmly placing the last of the papers down, and looked James over in a slow perusal. "How long have you been designing for Skye Designs?" he asked, his tone smooth and level.

"About five years. I assure you, I am not new to this, if that's concerning you."

Seth made no comment to James's nervous worry. "And the work you were doing when I came to collect you, may I see it now?"

As much as James didn't want to hand over the sketchbook, something about the way Seth asked made it impossible for him to say no. He was careful as he maneuvered over to his pack and drew it open, retrieving his work, rough though it was, and handed it over without meeting Seth's eyes. He didn't let others view his work until it was done. While he still drew and painted, no one saw his true art anymore. Not since he'd given it up to *get a real job* and *be a man*.

Seth opened the pad and examined the drawings within. He didn't stay on just the one sketch, but began turning the pages. James couldn't tell what Seth thought of the sketches since he kept his face too well controlled.

After what seemed to James to be an eternity, Seth sat the pad down and looked at him. "Get your things, we're going to go get something to eat, then we will discuss the designs and this," he finished and tapped the sketchbook. Without waiting for any response, Seth gathered up the materials, setting them on his desk, then grabbed his coat, phone, and keys.

James stood staring for a moment, baffled by the man's actions as much as his words. "Um, sir, there's no need to feed me. If you need time to think over the design needs or to collaborate with the others, I understand and can return next week."

A small smile played at the edges of Seth's lips, which drew his attention, making him even more aware of Seth's natural sensuality. *He probably doesn't even realize how breathtaking he really is.*

"James, we both need to eat, so unless you have somewhere you need to be right now, why not eat with me?"

His calm and matter-of-fact way of putting it made James agree before he had really even thought to respond. "Okay," he said, but it sounded more like a question to his own ears.

After they loaded everything into James's CRV, Seth's car service picked them up. With only a little pushing, he was able to convince Seth to tell him where they were going, Bacchus—an expensive, five-star restaurant on the waterfront.

James attempted to protest but was silenced when Seth gave him a quelling look. "I said I'm hungry, you're accompanying me to dinner, and this is where I wish to eat. When it's your turn, you may pick the place."

It had been ages since he'd gone out to any place like Bacchus, even before Victor, since he hated places like that, making fun of their refinements. *Wait, did he just say "your turn"?* Both James's heart and mind seemed to trip at the thought of more alone time with the delicious Mr. Seth Burns.

"They have exquisite seafood and an extensive wine list. I'm sure you will find something that meets your tastes," Seth explained as they were seated at a private table near the back—at Seth's request.

After ordering his drink, James debated what to order—hiding behind his menu really. When their server reappeared with the drinks, inquiring about their order, Seth arched an eyebrow at James. "Trust me?" he asked. James felt so overwhelmed all he managed was a slight nod, fearing his voice would crack if he spoke. "Good."

Turning back to the server, he spoke again. "Yes, I'll have the spinach salad followed by the tuna au poivre and the gentleman will have the roasted sweet potato salad with the grilled Scottish salmon."

Once they were alone again, James spoke up. "I could have ordered for myself, you know." He wasn't damaged like that; he could take care of himself!

As if reading his thoughts, Seth chuckled. "Relax, I know you can. I simply enjoy caring for my dinner dates. I assure you, your interestingly colored accessories do not impair my opinion of you, or your abilities," he added. The look Seth gave him went straight to his groin, causing his comfortable slacks to become rather tight.

"Now, I want to know more about your art," Seth continued.

"Okay. Which of the designs are you and your team leaning towards? Once I have that, I will work on the full mock-ups and a wider range of modifications to fit your needs." James was glad to be back on even footing. Work, design—that was safe. Comfortable.

"I need a little more time to make that decision. I was actually referring to the rather extraordinary *sketches* I saw in the book of yours. Where do you show?"

James's mind went blank for a moment. *Show?* He almost choked, thankful for the temporary distraction as their salads arrived. After taking a few bites—*wow, that's good*—he responded, though more in response to Seth's piercing stare rather than anything he'd said. "I—I don't. Not anymore," he said, worrying the edge of his cloth napkin.

"Why not? What I saw, some of those rough sketches, as you call them, could be sold as is, now. For a nice sum I might add. The passion and sensuality in even the more mundane images speak to the soul, not just the eyes. I can't imagine what a finished work would feel like if those are your roughs," Seth explained.

His words stirred something within James's soul, something he'd thought gone forever. "I had to grow up, get a real job. I enjoy art but...." He trailed off, not sure how to continue. He'd done the responsible thing so he could take care of his little family, even if his being with Victor had been a huge waste of time—and nearly cost him his life.

Seth made a humming noise as he seemed to mull over what James had said. James tried to ignore him, returning to his salad.

He was thankful when Seth moved the discussion to more mundane things once their entrees arrived, allowing him to relax and enjoy his meal. He even found himself enjoying the company, as strange as that seemed. James didn't date and rarely went out, even with friends, so this was new for him.

After ordering a fall pear torte to share, Seth looked him over with open interest. Though not leering, Seth made his interest known both with his attention and the gentle touches to the back of James's hand. "I would like to schedule a private showing of your art."

"Mr. Burns."

"Seth, please. We're not at work so no need for such formalities, especially when out with me like this," he finished with a devilish smile.

"Seth, I told you, I don't show anymore," James countered, wondering about the look of interest in Seth's eyes, or what he thought was interest. He had trouble believing what he thought he saw.

"Now, James, I didn't ask for a public show. I said I would like a private viewing of your work. I assume you have a studio still, and you obviously still have the gift if what I saw was any indication. I'd like to see the finished products."

"I, um, I suppose I could let you see a couple of my paintings, but my studio is attached to my home," he explained, fidgeting again. He hadn't shown his work in ages, not since using some of it in his portfolio to land the job at Skye Designs.

"Good. Then you'll let me know when you're available and I will stop by. Better yet, I'll be busy with the hotel next week, and have to go out of town for a few days. Do you think you would be free to do the viewing next Saturday? It would give you time to think about which ones you would like to show and have them set up. I'm not asking for anything new, so that should be plenty of time."

James agreed, his mind swirling with ideas and plans of what to show, how to best display in his small studio.

Once they returned to where he left his car, he went to slide out, reaching for his crutches, when Seth stopped him. Touching his face in a gentle caress, Seth leaned in and ghosted his lips across James's before wishing him a good night.

James was too stunned to do more than move from one car to the other. He reached up to touch his lips once Seth's car had pulled away. They tingled and he could taste the faint sweet and spice from their dessert with something more underneath, something he hoped he would get a chance to taste again.

chapter three

THE week passed excruciatingly slow, and yet it seemed to pass in a blink. When James wasn't at work, he was either painting or obsessing over what to show and how. The sketch he had done while waiting that fateful Friday had possessed him all weekend. He thought it might even be done by his showing on Saturday. Wednesday night, he made the mistake of calling Chase to ask his advice, and after a lot of noise and innuendos, he'd come over to help set things up for him.

"I don't know why you don't show your stuff publicly. I mean, I bet a lot of this would sell, Jamie. Especially if you had the right audience," Chase said as he helped move and place things.

"You know why I stopped, Chase," James said as evenly as he could manage.

"Yes, and he's an ass you need to finish getting over. Putting his lying, abusive ass out isn't enough. You need to delete that soundtrack he left in your head too. Your work is good, really good. You're an artist, no matter what he said." Chase continued his admonishments as he worked. He kept trying to peek behind the tarp James had used to block his work in progress from view. Patience was not one of Chase's blessings. "Ah, come on, Jamie, please," he begged. "Just a little peek?"

"Chase, the answer was no an hour ago, half an hour ago, ten minutes ago, and guess what? It's still no. It's not quite finished and this one's special."

"Fine," Chase pouted. "Deny me my little joys," he sniffed.

"You make a great drama queen, my dear, but the answer is still no. I need to finish it first. Now, are you done moving things?" James asked, moving back to take in the effect of his displays. *Yes, I think that's it! Now to finish up and not totally lose it beforehand.*

He was almost late Friday morning since he'd overslept, thanks to staying up late with Chase and working feverishly to finish the painting. He'd done it though! With a light heart and a sense of accomplishment he hadn't felt in years, he dressed and headed out for his last day of work before Seth stopped by. That had been the other reason he was up so late the last two nights. Chase had insisted they clean the whole house, convinced it might "come in handy," so he came back over Thursday night to clean. James had a cleaning service that came every week, and he was a pretty tidy guy, but Chase had been adamant.

Thankful that Seth picked Saturday, James did his normal shopping that morning before physical therapy, which gave him a little time to recover before the private showing that afternoon.

When the doorbell rang, his heart stopped for a moment before picking up and beating double-time. He opened the door and was dumbfounded by the sight before him. Seth stood there smiling, a huge bouquet of flowers held in his arms. Just at a glance James realized it was more than a dozen long-stem rainbow roses in a frosted lavender vase.

"Uh, what are those for?" James asked, mystified by the sweet gesture. He'd never been given flowers, especially from a client. Well, other than the get-well bouquets when he was in the hospital after the "accident," but those were normal. This was not.

"I saw them and thought of you and your art. I didn't know if you had a vase so I got this one," Seth explained. Passing through the foyer, he looked around the great room, taking in the cathedral ceiling, and sauntered over to the antique accent table against one wall. He rearranged things a little before he carefully placed the vase upon it.

James still stood with the door open. He blinked, staring at his strange guest. "Thank you," he said, once he snapped out of his daze and closed the door.

"I'd like a tour, if you don't mind, James. Before the reveal, of course."

James couldn't get over the command in everything Seth did or said, the way he took over. In a way, it felt natural and safe to him, not manipulative or degrading. Without much thought, he gave Seth a short tour of his home. It was a decently sized one-level stone cottage-style home that originally had four bedrooms, two of which were master sized. The second master bedroom he'd had converted into his studio, adding a door to the outside. A large bay window made it open and airy yet still protected his work. All the windows had a special UV coating, which protected his paintings from the sun.

When they entered the studio, James's nervousness nearly caused him to stumble. He kept telling himself it didn't matter what Seth thought, but he knew he was lying to himself. He did care, more than he probably should.

Seth didn't say anything for a long time, just wandered from place to place, examining James's art; truly his very soul was bound up in those images of lust, pain, loss, and joy. When Seth arrived at the tarp he'd left up, blocking his newest painting, James held his breath. It was complete, but the idea of showing it made him nauseous.

"James, what's behind this one?" Seth asked, his voice soft, almost a purr.

"It's the one you saw the sketch of last week. I, um, I finished it last night," he explained, knowing what was coming.

Without another word, Seth reached up and removed the tarp. He didn't look at the painting until he had taken the time to fold and set aside the material. James debated if he was just being neat or if Seth was deliberately trying to drive him nuts.

The man-sized canvas had been set up with key lighting to accentuate the images, making the hauntingly sensual images stand out even more. You could feel the desire, the aching need of the body splayed out on the bed, reaching for a lover who was just out of reach. The bedding pooled around him as if it was water, an ocean between the lovers.

"Come here, James," Seth commanded, his voice soft as it wrapped around James and drew him in. Once James stood in front of him, Seth murmured, "Who's the lover in the distance? And, why don't you believe you can have him?"

"It's not—"

"It is you, James. It is how you see yourself. I knew that last Friday." Trailing his strong hands down James's shoulders and arms, he leaned in and whispered against his ear, "Who is it that you seek, and why can't you have him?"

He froze under Seth's hands, failing to stop the tremble in his body as Seth's breath puffed against his ear. "Why can't he have you, baby?"

Trying to remember how to breathe, James shuddered again, unable to answer because he knew his answers would sound pathetic to the gorgeous man behind him. When he thought he might be able to speak again, he felt soft but firm lips press against the nape of his neck, just before a slight nip. He moaned, unable to restrain the sound or his body's reaction.

"I... I...."

"It's okay, for now. You aren't ready to answer those questions. I understand. But James," Seth said as he moved to stand before him and traced his fingers down James's cheek and jaw. "You will answer them soon."

James nodded, both his mind and body overwhelmed by Seth's words and touch.

Seth's eyes softened as he looked over James. After a moment he pulled back his hand and spoke again. "Come, let's lighten the mood a bit. Why don't I order us dinner? We can discuss your art and which pieces I'd like to purchase."

James took a moment to center his emotions after the abrupt change in direction before answering. "Um, sure. You don't have to feed me again, though. I mean, this is my home. I do have food here."

"Yes, but I'm hungry and I doubt you know how to make Indian, and that's what I'm craving. Well, part of what I'm craving anyway," Seth added. The look in his hazel eyes made James wonder if he wasn't also on the menu. But, even with all the touching, looks, and words, he still couldn't believe Seth could really want *him*.

THEY kept the conversation light as they ate. Seth stated there were three pieces he wanted, in addition to the newest one, of course. Once dinner was over, James went to clean their dishes. He was almost finished when he felt hands on his hips. He turned and stood rooted to the spot as Seth's gaze swept over him and sent tingles through his body that seemed to settle in his groin. "You—"

"You're beautiful, you know," Seth said, cutting off James's nervous attempt to play off his attraction to the first man he'd wanted in years. "Like sex and a perfect sunrise wrapped up in one." Tilting his head, Seth kissed him. It started softly, just barely touching the edge of James's mouth. Warm breath feathered across his face.

Seth sprinkled kisses across his jaw, slowly moving to whisper in his ear, "I've wanted you since I first saw you, James." Seth pulled his head back and kissed him again, but this time with possession, not the light, sensual assault from before. His muscles tightened in response to the possessive, demanding invasion of his senses. Their tongues teased and wrapped around one another; lips were nibbled and licked.

James felt Seth grasp his hips and pull him flush against him. He aligned their hips and pressed into James's throbbing erection. He was almost surprised to feel how hard Seth was. He closed his eyes and embraced Seth, and pushed him back against the wall. He couldn't stand long unassisted but was determined to make the most of Seth's temporary insanity. Kissing Seth again, he allowed his lips to travel down the long column of his neck. Leaning against him, he pulled Seth's shirt up so he could touch more skin.

"That feels so good, baby," Seth murmured.

James sank to his knees and slid his hands slowly to coast up the fronts of Seth's thighs. Seth closed his eyes and dropped his head forward as the touch slid up and down his legs to stop at his waistband. "James, you don't have to," Seth murmured as he shuddered under the sensual touches.

Ignoring the whispered words, he peeled Seth's underwear and jeans down in one motion. He leaned forward, his hands instinctively going to Seth's hips. He inhaled Seth's scent, the musky, spicy odor of his aroused partner, at least for tonight. Flicking his tongue out, he caught the glistening pearl of moisture from his slit. When he put his mouth on him, he thought about nothing but the cock, the man in front of him.

Stretching his lips and jaw with the size and length before him, he slid down, down, down. He relaxed his muscles to take him deeper, until the wide head popped into his throat, cutting off his air. James let out a groan as his lips brushed against the soft nest of curls that surrounded Seth's root. He couldn't help the needy little noises that vibrated against Seth's head as he slowly skated up his length, and created suction as he slid through his lips. He traced his tongue down the pulsing vein under the crown.

Seth's hand convulsed at the nape of James's neck as he let out a deep growl. "God. Don't stop!" he said, and let his head thunk back against the wall. James paid special attention to the sensitive area just under the crown. He sucked and lightly grazed the pulsing cock with his teeth—just enough to pull him to the edge of pain and pleasure, but not enough to hurt.

"James…," Seth breathed. James released a guttural moan as he sucked harder. Cheeks hollowed, he flicked and swirled against the sensitive underside with his tongue as he tugged teasingly on Seth's sack with his fingers.

Sliding up and down Seth's dripping cock, James set the rhythm, but backed off when he felt Seth's balls raise and tighten. He didn't want it to end, not yet. Through glazed eyes, he gazed worshipfully up at Seth and murmured, "I want."

Even though James couldn't seem to articulate any better, Seth seemed to understand the nearly silent plea. He kicked off the pants James had nearly divested him of before. Bending down, he scooped James up into his arms, wrapped James's legs around his hips, and carried him out of the room. Before James knew what was happening, he found himself being lowered to the edge of his large oak bed. Seth stepped back, looked at James for a moment before he peeled off his shirt.

James swallowed hard, still afraid this might be a dream. Before the flutter in his gut could distract him, Seth skimmed his hands over his shoulders, and settled on the top button of his shirt. Leaning in to kiss James, he unbuttoned James's shirt while he pushed him back onto the bed. Each time he exposed more, Seth would caress or kiss the skin. Once the shirt was open, he took his time as he kissed his way back up to James's small nipples. Drawing the hardened bud into his mouth, he flicked it with his tongue before lightly biting down.

"Ungh," James groaned as he arched up into Seth's ministrations, hoping it would never end.

"Shh," Seth soothed, returning his lips to James's. Pulling him up only long enough to remove the shirt, Seth increased the intensity of the kisses as he settled his weight onto him. Without thought, James shifted, letting Seth settle into the vee of his thighs. He wished he was naked so he could feel Seth's skin on his but was distracted when Seth's lips and teeth latched onto his throat, worrying the flesh, and drove all thoughts from his mind.

"Hope you don't mind," Seth murmured against his collarbone, not that James could have articulated a complaint if he had one. All he seemed able to do was squirm and moan, rocking his hips up as Seth locked his lips around James's nipple. He was certain he was going to spontaneously combust or lose his mind if Seth didn't stop his sensual, driving assault.

Seth stopped, pulled back to look at his handiwork. He seemed pleased with the vibrant marks James knew he'd left on his throat and chest. "Damn you're sexy," he said, voice rough with desire.

James couldn't stop the whine when Seth stood up and broke contact with his overheated flesh. "Don't worry, baby, I just want to feel more of you," he explained as he reached down to tug open James's jeans. His eyes devoured James as his cock sprang free of the black cotton boxer-briefs under the denim material.

Seth didn't touch James as he removed the rest of his clothes and tossed them somewhere across the room. "I'm going to love showing you what our bodies can do together, baby."

"God," James groaned, and shivered hard when Seth ran the tip of one finger up the underside of his cock, tracing the large vein. "Don't tease, Seth!"

When he finally grasped James's cock, Seth gave a single, powerful stroke before he ran his thumb through the viscous liquid seeping from its slit. As he brought his thumb to his own lips, he licked the precome from it, his eyes never leaving James's. Before he could blink, Seth had engulfed him in the most wondrous wet heat he'd ever felt.

"Oh God," he yelled, his hips coming up off the bed. It took all his willpower not to release down Seth's throat. It was only the understood promise of more that let him hold back. He spread his legs wider, a silent plea for more. Bobbing his head, Seth maintained the moist heat and suction on his cock until James cried out. "Not yet," he whimpered. He was desperate to get Seth to stop before he lost it and released despite his wants for more. He shook with the effort to stop. Instead of backing off completely, Seth moved down so he could nuzzle James's sack. He licked and sucked gently until James was rocking and shaking, begging for more.

Pushing James's legs up, Seth's tongue flicked across his taint until he reached his tight, quivering pucker. James had never felt anything like it before. Seth's tongue licked and stabbed at him, opening him in the most incredible way. He moaned and rocked as he was consumed by the most amazing sensation ever. James chanted *Oh God,* and *please,* and *fuck me,* over and over as Seth continued his sensual assault.

James's mind completely shut down as Seth worked a finger into his body next to the tongue that continued to fuck him. Suddenly the tongue and finger left, but before he could focus, a slicked finger returned and pressed back inside his body. He felt Seth's other hand wrap around his cock, stroking in rhythm with the finger.

"Seth…. Please, God!" James knew he was babbling but didn't care, as Seth continued to go deeper until his finger found James's sweet spot. When he hit it, it sent jerking shocks of pleasure through James. After only moments, the finger was joined by another. The slight burn dissipated quickly and transformed into the most incredible and overpowering sensations. After a time, two became three, plunging into him and scissoring as Seth continued to stretch him for what was to come.

The bed shifted as Seth reached past him with the hand that had stroked him. James heard the drawer to his nightstand open and close. The penetration never stopped, though. James watched in wonder as Seth sheathed his cock with a condom, and whimpered as Seth slicked up his thickness before he maneuvered his cock to James's opening. His fingers slid out only for James to feel the head of Seth's cock touch his hungry opening. "Don't tense up, baby, because I'm going to fuck you until I'm the only man you can remember ever touching your amazing body," Seth ordered with a growl that shot straight to James's core.

"Fuck!" James cried as Seth pressed into his body. He stretched and filled James's body as it never had been before. James forgot to breathe for a moment as Seth continued to push in, not stopping until he was fully seated, overwhelming James completely. While he stopped to let James catch his breath and adjust to his size, he draped James's legs over his shoulders. True to his word, Seth didn't give him time to think, pulling almost all the way out before he slid back in forcefully. James grasped at Seth's shoulders and arms for purchase, and his head rolled back and forth as he moved to meet Seth's punishing thrusts. The sensations were so powerful they seemed to penetrate to his very soul. He knew he wouldn't last but didn't want to go over alone.

"Harder. More, damn it," James demanded.

Trembling against the bedding, fists tightly gripping the sheets, James barely managed to keep himself from screaming as he begged for this night, and Seth's exquisite torture of his body, to never end.

"Not gonna last," he gasped out. Desperate to have Seth come with him, he tightened his muscles and gripped the invading cock. A moment later Seth slammed into him and held still as he roared his release. James cried out as he felt the throbbing inside him. It pushed him over the edge, painting their chests and stomachs with his hot seed. Seth collapsed on top of him and clutched James as though he might float away. They shook together, calming and breathing until they could think and move again.

After an indeterminate amount of time, Seth slipped from his body, eliciting a disappointed groan from James. "Don't move," Seth said softly. He then padded quietly to the ensuite bathroom and returned with a warm washcloth. He gently cleaned James's chest, abdomen, cock, then bottom before he tossed the cloth toward the door and climbed back into the bed with him. Seth reached out, rolled James to his side facing away, and curled up behind him, spooning as he stroked James's hair softly.

"You are the most amazing man, James," Seth said as James wiggled backward, settling more firmly into the crook of Seth's body.

James tried to focus his thoughts through the euphoria of everything they had done together, but before he could speak, Seth spoke. "Don't. I can feel you tensing, James. Rest here with me and when you wake up, you can worry about clothes and propriety. For right now, you're mine and I don't intend to sleep alone. Now, go to sleep, baby. The morning will be here soon enough."

Sated, warm, and feeling oddly safe, James did just that.

chapter four

AS HE rolled over, James was immediately reminded of his activities the night before. Sore? Yes, but in the most delicious of ways. Seth had woken him twice, leaving him filled and satisfied in ways he'd never felt, hadn't even dreamt of before. Every thought of the commanding and passionate ways Seth had taken him made James shiver.

Cracking one eye open, he expected to see Seth beside him, but what he found was an empty spot. When he touched the sheets he realized they were cold. Seth had been gone a while. Bitter disappointment settled over him as he thought about what it meant to awake alone in a cold bed.

"Knew he was too good to be true," he grumbled. His mood and outlook on the day soured, and it wasn't even eight yet.

James tried to go back to sleep but Seth's scent surrounded him, teased his senses, and reminded him of how stupid and easy he'd been. *Seth got what he wanted, why bother sticking around?* At least his aches were from something pleasant rather than what he'd experienced with Victor. Shutting down that train of thought, he decided to get out of bed and try to start his day. He'd just forget about last night and pretend it didn't happen. He would not lose his job or this account over what, it seemed, meant nothing to Seth.

After a long, hot shower, James dressed in jeans and a simple T-shirt. He ignored his reflection, which showed the vivid proof of his activities the night before, not wanting to dwell on his being alone again. Foregoing any footwear, he maneuvered with his worn, paint-splattered crutches, the ones he used when painting, to the kitchen. He decided he would eat something and then put his pain and disappointment into his art instead of sitting around brooding all day. *Might as well use my stupidity for something, right?*

He grabbed a glass of juice, but startled when he entered the breakfast nook and saw Seth standing on the patio with his back to him, a takeout coffee cup in hand, as he looked out over the woods behind the little stone cottage. His shirt billowed slightly behind his body and pulled across his powerful shoulders. The slacks he wore sat low on his hips, as if they might not be fully zipped and buttoned in front. As the breeze kicked up, James couldn't help but catch glimpses of Seth's firmly muscled back, making his mouth water even as he warred with himself over thoughts of his previous assumption.

He couldn't help but stare. He'd been so sure Seth had used and discarded him. The urge to rush over, touch him, make sure he wasn't some apparition instead of the most beautiful man he'd ever met welled up inside him.

James must have made some sound, because Seth turned, a gentle smile on his lips. "Good morning, pet," he said as he entered the nook to join James. "Since you're awake now, I'll make you breakfast. What would you like in your omelet?"

"You're still here," he blurted. He felt like an idiot and wished he could take it back as soon as the words left his mouth.

"Of course, James. Where else would I be?" Seth said with a chuckle that settled deep in his soul. "Now, toppings?"

"Mushrooms, bell peppers, and cheese?" He thought he had bought some of each yesterday, though his memories prior to Seth's arrival were a little muddy. "But, you don't need to cook. I can do that."

"I know you can, that's not an issue. I want to pamper you. Now, sit down," Seth said in a tone of command that shot straight to his cock. *Why does that tone make me want him so bad?*

James found himself doing as ordered, and sat at the bar so he could watch Seth move around his open kitchen like he owned it. "I picked up a few things when I went out earlier, you didn't have everything I wanted," Seth explained as he chopped and sautéed the veggies before adding them to the omelets.

"Set the table, pet. I'm almost done."

Again, James found himself doing as told. He hadn't realized it wasn't a request but yet another command until he was done. Seth brought out two plates with fluffy, overstuffed egg white omelets and fresh fruit. "I can't stay all day as I would like to, but I wanted to take care of you a little before I have to go."

"I understand, thank you. This is delicious," James said, curious about where Seth had to go on a Sunday. He tried not to let it bother him, especially since he hadn't expected to even have this time with Seth, not after waking alone. He wished this could be a real, normal relationship, like healthy people got to have, though.

"I'll also have the movers stop by tomorrow after you get home to pick up the paintings we discussed last night," Seth explained. "I still need to settle on prices with you, but I disagree with what you quoted. I know it's a Sunday but I'll have Mel stop by today to have them appraised both for price and insurance so you don't have to worry about it and work schedules. Do you have plans later? I need to let Mel know when to come over."

Feeling suddenly indignant, James replied, "The prices I quoted you are more than fair, Seth. These aren't knockoff prints or something. I know I'm not famous or something but—"

"Enough," Seth said in such a tone as not only stopped him from speaking, but made him pull back suddenly. He hadn't meant to upset or insult Seth, but his art was his life and soul. He had thought Seth understood.

"Do you think I was arguing that you were trying to charge me too much?" The tone and way Seth held himself left James mute and fearful that he might not be as gentle a person as he had thought. All he managed was a nod, scared that anything he said would be wrong somehow. He knew that dance; it had landed him on the floor, against the wall, even in ICU once.

"I," he managed to squeak out.

Suddenly Seth was beside James, stroking his hair as he pulled James's head against his abdomen. "Shh... baby. You're okay. That's not why I want Mel to come over. He's a lawyer, but his wife runs a gallery in town. I think you're underpricing your work, not overpricing.

"Here." Picking up James's abandoned fork, he scooped up a small bite and fed it to James. "You need to eat. You're too skinny." He continued to feed James until the plate was finished. He stood so he was over James, gently sheltering him with his body. James was baffled by the gesture and by Seth's overall attitude and behavior. He also wondered why he was being fed.

Once breakfast was over, Seth let James help with the clean up. That was the best way he could describe it, as being *allowed* to help. No one ever helped at home, not like that. He had bought the cottage after he'd had Victor removed from his old apartment the last time, so it was his and his alone. Chase picked up after himself when he was over and had helped clean for the past couple of days, but even that had been a first. He was so confused but could not help but acquiesce to Seth's demands and instructions.

"Do you really have to go?" James found himself asking as he dried and put away the last dish. He didn't want their bubble in time to burst, didn't want to lose the contentment and joy he had found in Seth's arms, even though he knew Seth would never settle for someone like him for long. It was a pleasant fantasy he wasn't ready to give up.

"I do, and as much as I hate to do it this way, I will be gone for about two weeks. My plane leaves this evening so I must go for now. Mel and Brittany will stop over this afternoon about the art. I hope to have it in its new home before I return.

"Look at me," he commanded, as he noted James's down-turned face. "I will call you this week and we can talk some. When I get back, I want us to go out somewhere nice. I will let you know when I decide where that will be. Also, you will work with Sandy while I'm gone. I hate the timing but it is what it is.

"Now, give me a kiss and walk me out, baby," he said. Heat flashed in his eyes as he pulled James against him and took possession of his mouth in a bruising, nearly violent kiss that made James think, once he could again, that maybe, just maybe, Seth really would come back and pick things up with him.

He stood on the front porch and watched Seth leave. He finally got to see his personal car, and what a car. It was a brand-new metallic-moonlight-blue Audi A7. As Seth drove away, James noticed the license plate, which read PROUD.

JAMES tried to focus on sketching but jumped at every car that passed, nervous about meeting Seth's friends, especially alone. He was also worried about Brittany, Mel's wife, since Seth had said she ran a gallery. What if she hated his work? Victor had said it wouldn't sell well, that it wasn't good enough, and he'd nearly given up painting. But, considering how Seth had looked at the pieces he'd chosen, maybe Vic had been wrong about that too. He tried to squash the anticipation he felt, not wanting to get his hopes up again.

By late afternoon, he'd fallen into his work and lost himself completely in it until his doorbell startled him back to reality. He quickly put his tools down and hurried to answer it, and realized he was speckled almost as much as his crutches as he opened the door.

A petite brunette in a short black slip dress and what had to be five-inch heels stood next to a nice-looking older blond man. He was dressed more casually, though no less expensively. The man held his hand out and said, "You're James, right? I'm Mel, Mel Holcomb, and this is my wife, Brittany. Seth said you were expecting us." James quickly shook both their hands before inviting them in.

"Sorry I'm such a mess, I guess I got kinda distracted in the studio," James said as looked down at himself again.

Brittany laughed. "You're an artist, dear. I'd be concerned if you weren't covered in your preferred medium, which I see is a mix of oil and acrylics," she added, as she looked at his hands and hair carefully.

"Well, er, yes, it is in this case. I needed the different mediums for what I'm working on. Can I get you a drink or anything?" he continued as he led them through the great room, pausing at the entrance to the kitchen. They both declined, so he led them on to his studio.

"It's a little bit of a mess over near the window-wall, but the works Seth said he wanted are over here." He led them to the other side of the room where the pieces were still set up. He had re-hung the tarp to separate the area and to protect against any possible damage to the completed pieces.

She waved him off, wandered through his artwork, and stopped to look at each as she sized them up. When she got to the most recent, the one Seth wanted most, she stopped and gasped. "Mel, is this it? The one Seth gave special instructions for? Please say it's not because I want it," she said emphatically.

"Ma'am, that one is special and the primary painting he requested. It's already been bought, even if we haven't agreed on the price, yet," James explained before Mel had a chance to reply.

"Britt, you know full well that's the one he wants, and you won't win a bid war with Seth. Hell, no one wins against him. Ever. Now, be good and tell the nice man that he's undercharging like Seth said, then you can try to buy from him if you want," Mel said, and struggled to not laugh. He mostly succeeded.

With the prettiest pout James had ever seen on an adult, she turned to face him. "He's right. Seth told me what you asked for each of the pieces and I could get at least ten times that at the gallery, especially if they were featured in our next auction or show. Okay, so maybe that's a conservative estimate. Still, if you're this good, why aren't you in at least one gallery? Say, mine?" she said, eyes wide.

They spent the next hour or so discussing and debating what he had already promised to Seth and her desire for him to show at her gallery. By the time they left, he had a check for what he considered a ridiculous amount signed by Mel as Seth's attorney, and a consignment contract for six other paintings. He also had the schedule for the moving specialists that would be by to collect the paintings and deliver them for Brittany and Seth.

He couldn't believe what had happened and so, as always, he called Chase.

JAMES heard from Seth Monday evening. The call was short and mostly to check and make sure the transfer went as planned. By Friday, having not heard from him again, James started to doubt Seth's sincerity of their one night being a start for them. He knew he sounded like a whiny teen girl wondering why some boy didn't call the morning after, but he couldn't help it. Seth was the first man to really turn his head in years, the first to show any interest, well, for more than a quickie, which he always turned down flat. He would rather be alone than used, though that was how he was starting to feel again.

Friday, as they got ready to leave the office, Chase cornered him. "Come on, I can't stand to see you moping around like this. We're going out and have some fun."

"You know I don't like bars, Chase. I got knocked down last time we went out by some stupid drunk," James said as he attempted to escape, but knew it was futile even as he spoke. Chase had never learned the word "no."

An hour later, they were seated at a small corner table at Chase's favorite gay bar, with a snifter full of brandy, and tried not to be in the way. That only lasted until trouble walked in the door. Victor spotted them about the same time James saw him. He tried not to cringe, but the panic was hard to fight. Every time he saw Victor, the "accident" ran through his mind in excruciatingly painful detail, both what caused the wreck and the aftermath.

He grabbed Chase's arm and squeezed as he ground out, "Go. I've got to leave, Chase."

But before he could do more than get to his feet with his crutches, Victor was at their table, his thick finger jabbing James's chest. "You never were worth a damn and even now, all you are is a waste. What the hell did you say to that Seth guy, Jay? You cost me my spot on the crew, damn you!" Victor yelled, and drew the attention of a few people, including one of the bouncers. Unfortunately for James, his panicked squeak pushed Victor over the already precarious edge he rode, and with a crack, the world went black. He faintly remembered pain, he thought in his face and chest, but the black waters dragged him under too fast to be certain.

BEEP Beep Beep

God, what is that infernal noise? James wondered as he slowly became aware of his surroundings. It hurt to open his eyes, and when he did, he wished he hadn't. *Hospital,* he thought and groaned.

"Shh... Jamie," he heard Chase whisper. A soothing hand rubbed lightly up and down one arm. "I know you hate these places but you're safe."

James heard something click next to him just before a disembodied female voice asked what they needed. The next little while was a blur as nurses and a doctor came in, poked at his ribs, and asked questions he either didn't know how or didn't have the focus to answer. He was so thankful Chase was there, because his mind was useless right then.

Finally things died down and a cop in uniform came in, and asked, "James Bryant, right?"

"Yes."

"I'm Officer Holmes. I've gotten the statements from your friend as well as a bouncer, a bartender, and a few patrons of the bar you were in, but I need to know what you remember," the cop said, his voice gentle. "I hate having to ask so soon. I know you hurt. I've had my ribs cracked a time or two, but—"

"It's okay," he said, cutting off the cop's babbled apology. He then told what he remembered, which wasn't much.

Once he was finished, Chase added, "James has a protection order against Victor already. This isn't the first time he's attacked Jamie. You have to do something!"

"Calm down, sir. We have Mr. d'Leone in custody and with the witnesses and hospital report, it's a pretty clear case of felony battery." They spoke for a few more minutes, but the cop finally left, leaving Chase alone in the ER room with James.

"Jamie, I need you to think about something, and before you start, no, I don't think you're a cripple or any such stupidity," Chase said with a snort. "But, you can't use your crutches for a few days. Besides the cracked ribs, look at your arm." James did as instructed and examined the arm Chase motioned toward. He must have tried to block either Vic's punches or kicks, because his right arm was swollen and discolored. He feared to see what his heavily bandaged hands looked like. He was sure once the painkillers wore off, it would hurt like a mother.

"Before you freak out, it's not broken. I don't know why though—those were steel-toed boots—but you're going to be in a chair for a couple of days."

"What about my hands, Chase? What's wrong with them?" He could hear how his voice raised, but if his hands were destroyed, so was he.

"Not broken, but some of your joints were badly dislocated. They're in temp braces under the wrappings."

"Will I—"

"Calm down, hun. They put your fingers back in place right, and you know how this works, your house is already accessible, but, well, I want to stay with you. I'll crash in your spare room, but I don't think you should be alone right now. Probably just for the weekend. Okay?" Chase looked at him with wide, pleading eyes. He knew how much James hated the wheelchair, though he still had one from his time recovering after the "accident."

"Fine," he sulked. He knew he was being childish, but under the circumstances, he didn't really care. "But your gossiping tendencies have to go on holiday, Chase. I don't want anyone that doesn't already know to find out. Maybe it'll heal up before Seth comes back. If he comes back," he added quietly. Chase either didn't hear his mumblings or chose to ignore them.

"I only gossip about sexy men in compromising positions, not about you getting hurt. You should know better," he added with a huff.

After a flurry of paperwork Chase had to sign for him, and instructions he was glad they also printed for him, as he would never remember them all, he was finally released from the E.R. and sent home.

chapter five

HE CALLED Carl, his senior manager, Monday morning and explained what had happened. After he had assured Carl he would be fine, he stayed home for the first part of the week.

By Thursday, James told Chase where to put the damn chair once he painfully made his way back to work on his crutches. So, Thursday was the first anyone other than Chase had seen him since the attack. He got a lot of stares and a few questions, but even Brian-the-dick left him alone.

That afternoon, James's cell rang, but instead of answering it, he sent it straight to voice mail. Chase, who had eaten lunch with him, refused to go away no matter how many times he said he was fine. He looked at the cell curiously and asked, "Who are you avoiding, Jamie?"

"It's nothing. Mind your own business."

"No, that was Seth's ringtone, wasn't it? This isn't the first time I've seen you shunt a call this week. Why aren't you answering? Last week you were moping over his not calling and now you won't answer. What gives?" Chase asked, sounding a little put out.

"He's been calling since earlier this week. I don't want to talk to him. It's probably just about his purchases or possibly the site designs, which I know Sandy already got his approval for since she faxed it over earlier."

"I can't let myself get attached again, Chase. I let that happen with Victor and look where it got me," he said, gesturing to the lurid bruises still on the side of his face. "Plus, how long would he really want me? It took him a week to call, so it's obvious that he's got other things to worry about."

"You're being an idiot. The most gorgeous man you've ever met is interested in you, is awesome in bed, or so you said, and you're worried he's bored after one night?" Chase snapped. "I'd pick up the phone before the first ring was done if it were me. I never get that lucky," he pouted.

"He can't make me care then leave if we don't ever really start. If he saw me right now, like he'd want anything to do with me? I didn't even fight back!" James nearly cried. He was hurt and all the old fears and pains were trying to drag him down into nothingness again. The fact that some of the damage from the attack was permanent wasn't helping. He awaited the delivery of his new silver finger-splints so he could do his work without screwing up his hands any worse. He couldn't stand to go through it again. While he didn't believe Seth would abuse him, not like Vic, he didn't believe he'd really want to stay either. He wasn't into one-offs or flings, no matter what it had appeared that night with Seth.

"Jamie, you're off in your head again. Talking it out works better, ya know and are you sure your hands won't heal?" Chase continued to badger James off and on all day, not letting up even on the ride home.

"Chase, you know full well that damage to joints doesn't fully heal with EDS. So yeah, I'm pretty sure," James snapped. Chase knew as much about his genetic disorder as he did, so why ask inane things like that? Seriously!

When his cell rang during dinner, Chase jumped up and answered it before James could send it to voice mail. What made it worse was he took off out the door, so James couldn't hear what was said. When Chase came back in, he returned the cell but refused to tell James anything about the conversation. Chase also left that night, returning to his home.

An on-site conference with Sandy the next morning meant he could sleep in, but he was tired, more mentally than physically. He decided to head to bed early so he could curl up and forget the last week or two.

STARTLED out of a sound sleep, James realized someone was knocking on his door—his outside bedroom door. "Chase, go home. I'm not interested in listening to you right now," he grumbled.

"Open the door, James" came the most beautiful yet icy voice he had ever heard.

"Seth? What the hell? It's—" He paused long enough to blink at the clock. "It's three in the morning and why are you even back?" He wasn't supposed to be there, was he?

"You will open this door, now. Then we will discuss why I am here at this ridiculous hour," Seth said with a voice like gentle steel. After grabbing his crutches, James stumbled to the door and flipped the lock.

"Fine, it's open. Now, go home and let me sleep," he nearly whined. He hadn't wanted Seth to see his bruises. *So much for wishes and intentions.* Without looking at Seth, he turned and headed back to his bed and sat on the edge. He hadn't turned up the light, so only the far lamp lit the room. He hoped it meant Seth wouldn't be able to see his injuries too well.

Seth sauntered in, headed straight for the wall where the light switch was, and flipped it, casting the entire room in harsh, bright light.

"Damn it, Seth. Warn a guy, would ya?" James snapped and blinked to disperse the bright spots in his vision.

Seth moved back to stand in front of him and peered down as anger flashed across his beautiful face before he controlled his expression again. "Why?" was all he said. He looked at James, obviously demanding an explanation in his usual, unusual way.

"It's not like I wanted this," James snapped, and turned away. He wished Seth would either leave or hold him; he couldn't decide which, and hated himself for that indecision.

"I never thought you did, baby," Seth murmured as he pulled James's stiff body into his arms and settled on the bed beside him. "You are submissive, not stupid. No, shh…," he soothed when James tried to pull away.

"I'm not like that," he said firmly. "I never liked what Victor did to me and I won't allow anyone else to ever do it again, not even you. He's in jail," James insisted. He'd heard that word used to describe him before, but it was Victor who had said it. He had even tried to convince James that the abuse was okay because it was what he had to do to keep James in line. He had only used that excuse late in their relationship, but James wasn't sure he ever wanted to hear that word again. Worse, though, it had come from Seth. Had he so misjudged the man? Had he let another abuser near him?

"Submission and abuse are not the same thing. This…," he continued, gently caressing James's hair to soothe him again. "What that monster did to you, I'd like to kill him for, but I will stay here with you instead since even I don't think I could get away with murder at the jail." He laughed, but it lacked any joy.

"I don't like being hurt, Seth. I didn't want to end up on crutches for the rest of my life, or in a wheelchair, for that matter. If that's what you're looking for, please leave. I can't do this again. I'll die before I go through that hell again!"

Turning James, he gently raised his face. Seth looked into his hollow eyes, releasing a muttered string of curses damning that son-of-a-bitch straight to the bowels of hell for what he had done to "such a treasure as James."

James's mind caught on the word treasure, wondering if Seth could actually see him that way.

"I swear this to you, James Bryant, I will never treat you like that. I will never leave your body broken and bloody like that ass did. Can you trust that I mean what I say?"

Looking into Seth's hazel eyes, captivated by what he saw—the power, the command of the man he knew he was falling for, stupidly he was certain—he also saw tenderness, and he thought maybe even honesty. Swallowing hard, James said, "Yes, I—I can try." He shook as he said the words, but something in him believed in Seth, even though his words terrified him.

"Good. Now, I should not have had to learn about the attack from Mel, nor should Chase have been the one to answer your phone or to send me pictures of your injuries."

James started to defend himself, but Seth cut him off. "No, I don't wish to hear excuses. You should have told me yourself, pet, but, under the circumstances, I will forget about it, this time. I expect you to answer your phone, though, especially when you know I'm supposed to call."

"I'm sorry," James said quietly. "I just didn't want you to see me like this. Chase has been through my hell before so that was okay, but—"

"But, you were afraid I would think less of you. For what, James? Put your fears aside for a moment, please. What did you have to fear from me that made you hide from a cell phone? It's a little pile of plastic," Seth said with a little shove. "Hardly intimidating."

"It wasn't the phone," James replied, smiling involuntarily. "I didn't want you to know I was this weak, that I couldn't manage to protect myself. It's bad enough you were there the day I panicked and tried to run out of the hotel. Not that you let me."

Seth leaned in, lightly brushed his lips against James's, and whispered warm breath and soft flesh across his mouth. "You are not weak, pet. You are an incredibly strong, sexy, passionate man that happens to have been attacked by a monster." He kissed James again, still gentle, placing a light kiss to each corner of his mouth before he traced James's lower lip with his tongue.

At that simple, light touch, James was hard and wanting. He startled when he realized the plaintive moan he heard had come from himself.

"Be careful, baby. I don't want to hurt you," Seth said, continuing to kiss and tease his lips, jaw, and neck.

"I'm fine," James murmured, and tried to increase the intensity and pressure of the kisses. Seth wouldn't have it, though. He kept firm control over the kiss, only intensifying it once James gave over control of their passion.

Gently, he pushed James back onto the bed, and stripped them both of all clothing before climbing into bed, carefully pulling James into his arms.

Seth did magical things to his body, pushing James's pleasure higher and higher with nothing more than his hands and mouth.

Sitting up against the head of the bed, Seth pulled James into his lap at an angle as he stretched his long legs out on either side of James's tight body. Wrapping his warm, strong fingers around James's cock, Seth set a slow, sensual pace, one that caused James to moan and writhe against him. "You need this, baby, but your body is still healing. You will stay still and let me take care of you," Seth instructed. His sultry steel-wrapped-in-silk voice slid over James, washing away his doubt and worry—at least for the moment.

Seth kept up the sensual torture until James's body throbbed, skin tingling everywhere. Finally, his other hand disappeared from James's sight but returned quickly. A couple of the fingers glistened as they descended below, reaching behind James's balls to lightly circle his opening before he slowly slid one inside. James hadn't even noticed the snick of the lube opening.

James moaned as his hips moved, shifting between increasing the slide of Seth's hand on his cock and forcing Seth's finger deeper within him. He couldn't seem to decide which he wanted more, but what he was certain of was his need to release soon.

After a few moments, he thought he'd go out of his mind with Seth's sexual assault, but then Seth carefully added a second finger and sped up his stroke.

As he kissed and nibbled on James's neck and ear, he whispered, "In a minute, I'm going to tell you to do something and you will do it. No questions, pet. Simply do as you're told." As he finished his murmured instructions, he increased the speed and grip of the hand shuttling on James's weeping, throbbing member just as he curled his other fingers deep inside to hit the sweet spot that would send electric jolts of divine pleasure throughout James's body.

When James thought he wouldn't be able to stop from coming, Seth softly commanded, "Come for me, pet. Now."

With those words and the single-minded focus on his cock and prostate, James couldn't do anything but come, as ordered. Arching up off Seth's chest, which drove the fingers even deeper, he felt the pulsing of his cock in that tight, nearly punishing grip as James shot stream after stream of hot, thick white seed over Seth's hand and his own stomach. It felt like his pleasure had been wrung from the very core of his being, forget just his body.

Seth gently continued to stroke James, to draw out his aftershocks until he started to whimper from over stimulation. Seth finally released him, wrapping both arms around him, seemingly thoughtful and aware of James's injuries, and rocked him slowly as he came back to himself.

JAMES found himself snuggled back into Seth as he floated on the haze of pleasure Seth had brought to his sore, battered body. He idly wondered how one man could make him feel safe, possessed, cared for, and wanted as he lay sated and content.

Seth eased him down slowly and stood, evidence of his arousal still exquisitely prominent. "Let me," James started to say.

"No, baby. You stay still. I'll be right back." Like their first night together, Seth headed to the ensuite, and brought back a warm cloth he used to clean James, his touch so soft it barely whispered across his tender skin. Once Seth climbed back in and curled around him, James tried to shift to touch Seth, but he tightened his arms around James, stilling his body.

"But you didn't. I mean," James said as he struggled for the right words. With Seth around, he seemed to frequently lose his ability to think or speak clearly.

"James, you need to rest. We will talk in the morning, when we have both had some rest." With those words, Seth pulled him tighter to his chest and held James until they both fell asleep.

STANDING in the doorway, Seth watched James sleep. He hadn't slept well in days, not since that first unanswered call, Monday. When Chase had answered James's cell and sent him the images of *his* James's bruised and battered body, he booked the first flight home, canceled the rest of his appointments and trip. He had used everything at his disposal to get back to his new pet as quickly as he could. Maybe he'd take James with him next time he needed to travel. *Wonder what he would think of that?* he thought with a wry smile.

James got up earlier, claiming he needed to go into the office before he headed to the hotel site. Seth had ordered him back to bed. He explained that since he was the client, he would call the office and let them know James would be on site, that way no one would notice his absence. In all actuality, James could move on to other projects now, only consulting with them from time to time for tweaks and special requests, a point Seth was not going to make known for as long as possible.

He liked watching James sleep, paint, hell, even the way James breathed turned him on. He only turned away when he heard the soft rap on the door. He hoped it was Dillon, his assistant. He had called him a little while before to give him a list of items he needed picked up and brought to James's little cottage. He liked his penthouse with all its amenities, but the stone cottage felt homey, sort of quaint and comfortable. He could see why James liked it so much.

Opening the door, he saw Dillon and a delivery driver he hadn't expected. He also saw a cop car pull up right behind his and park. Seth watched as Dillon hurried up the sidewalk with the UPS driver, and looked back at the two officers not far behind him.

He stepped aside as he let Dillon in but stepped back to block the passage when the driver and two officers finally arrived. They looked back and forth between each other and him before the UPS guy spoke. "Mr. Bryant?"

"No, I'm Seth Burns. James is resting right now. I'll sign for the delivery." The guy gave him no trouble and was quickly off, after a nervous look at the cops, and drove away.

"Now gentlemen, what can I do for you?"

The older officer spoke first. "We are here to speak with a James Bryant."

"He is still not well from his attack last weekend, officer. How may I help you?" He didn't want to upset or disturb James unless it was necessary. He had found out when James was up earlier that he had not been taking the pain medication prescribed, citing that it made him too sleepy and loopy to work. He handed him the pills and a glass of water and stood there until James gave in and took them. And sure enough, within half an hour, he was sleeping soundly again.

"That's why we're here, sir," the younger officer said. "I'm Officer Sayer and this is Officer Parks. The problem is more information and allegations have come to light and we need to speak with Mr. Bryant about those."

"Look, mister," the older one, Parks, said at Seth's reluctance. "I know he was hurt pretty badly. I saw the write-up. The problem is, Mr. d'Leone has lawyered up, of course, and now claims that while he may have gone a little—his words, not mine—overboard, it was James that attacked him first. There is a new bond hearing later today to reduce the bail amount and the responding officer is my brother-in-law. He asked us to come over and unofficially warn Mr. Bryant." Parks finished his speech, having said it all as if it was practically one long word.

With a hard sigh, Seth thought a moment before he pulled out his cell and gestured the officers inside. Twenty minutes later, Mel, his best friend since college and lawyer extraordinaire, sauntered in the door, just as James emerged from his room, dressed and mostly awake.

chapter six

JAMES sat at his kitchen table, unpacked his new silver ring splints, and fitted them onto his fingers and right thumb. He knew it drove Seth and Mel both crazy, but he needed to focus on something other than the questions that had come up thanks to the officers' visit. He knew they were trying to help, but reliving the horror his life had descended into off and on since he'd met Victor in college was not something he wished to do. To discuss any of that with Seth terrified him. So there he sat, adjusting his new rings as Seth and Mel paced and glowered.

"James, that is enough. You can fiddle with those, whatever they are, and talk at the same time. Mel needs to know things before the hearing and you are the best one to tell him," Seth snapped. His usual calm, commanding voice gave way to irritation and impatience. James found it amusing, though he kept that to himself.

With one last adjustment to the ring and bracelet on his right thumb, he finally looked up and met Seth's exasperated gaze. He raised his hands up to show off the rings he now wore, and explained, "These are my new splints, Seth. This is what Victor's kicking and stomping did. He damaged my joints and since I'm an artist, that's kind of a big deal for me. Now, I will answer what I can, but please, don't push if I say I don't know or can't tell you something."

Seth stilled and looked horror-struck. "You mean it's not just something you can heal from? Those don't look temporary, baby."

"They aren't. You never asked me why I use the forearm crutches. If you had, you would, maybe, understand that his attack was not just a little assault and battery—as if there was such a thing—but that he could have destroyed who and what I am, easily." James paused, afraid to talk, but knew he had to continue.

"James," Mel interrupted. "You can give Seth the long version later. Right now, I need the short one. Did you attack him? Does he know the dangers of whatever your condition is? What prompted his attack? And, can you provide me with any legal proof of his past actions? That's what we need to concentrate on, for now." He seemed so calm, it was almost comical compared to Seth's loss of composure.

"No. Yes. Seth getting him fired. And yes, in the files in my desk in the study," James answered. He knew it would likely irk them both, but he couldn't resist.

"James," Mel grumbled. "A little more detail would be helpful," he said, though James saw the smile he tried to hide.

"Fine. Yes, he knows. Early in our relationship he even went with me to the geneticist. I have a genetic disorder called EDS or Ehlers-Danlos Syndrome. It means the stuff that holds my joints together doesn't work right, amongst other things. There's a lot more to it, but for now, that should help you understand. It also means that when the joints are damaged they don't bounce back like a healthy person's does.

"The wreck he caused a few years ago nearly killed me and thanks to all the damage to my hips, knees, and pelvic structure, I use the crutches. The specialists thought I would be in the wheelchair permanently, but I refused to be defeated by that monster or their pessimism.

"What he did last Friday could have ended up with me losing my art and ability to walk even with the crutches. My fingers won't ever recover completely. These splints will help stop them from overextending and dislocating, though.

"As to proof." He feared what Seth would think and do. James left the room for a moment, bringing back a large tote filled with files and photos.

After he handed the tote to Mel, he looked back to Seth for the first time and explained. "I had to get a restraining order against him. I still have everything from that hearing. You should be able to pull the police records from when they removed him from my old apartment. There were a number of 911 calls throughout the years, but I never pressed charges until near the end when—" He choked on memories and couldn't continue.

"Shh, baby," Seth said, wrapped his arms around James, and tried to loan him some strength and support. "Mel, that has to be enough to show James is the victim, and not the aggressor. Well, between that and the firsthand witness accounts the officers mentioned."

Seth held him tightly, making him feel safe. James couldn't understand the strange sensations Seth brought about within him, not with his assumptions about Seth's previous relationships. He was still a little fixated on Seth's use of the word "submissive" and what he believed it meant. What Victor had said it meant.

"I pulled the records before, so, yes, I should be able to wrap this up. This is beyond just a bar fight. Considering their history and the restraining order, Mr. d'Leone is in contempt no matter who threw the first punch."

"I will call you later with an update. Seth." Mel paused, gave Seth a strange look, one James couldn't understand, then turned and left. No good-bye, nothing.

"Well, that was abrupt. Did I do something to upset your friend?" James asked.

Seth pulled James up and nudged the crutches into his hands. "No. Maybe one day he will tell you the story behind his behavior. Come sit with me, baby."

Seth led him back into his bedroom, and once they were settled against the headboard, Seth picked up one of James's hands and played with the new rings a little. "From the top, it just looks like you're really into rings," he noted.

"That's the point, Seth. I don't want to look broken. The crutches are bad enough, but the therapist said this was best if I wanted to keep drawing, painting, and all. Please tell me you don't care." The night before had meant so much to him. Not the sex part, though that had been wonderful, but the fact that Seth had come back early simply because James had been hurt. That brought him to tears once he had gotten over being pissed off at the self-righteous, arrogant, perfect man.

"Oh, I care, but not in the way you're worried about, pet. I care that someone hurt you. I care that you fear I would do the same. But I don't care about or respect you any less because of what you told us. You are even more amazing than I had thought."

AFTER work that evening, James eagerly anticipated his dinner out. He had insisted that he did, *in fact*, need to meet with Sandy at the new hotel site. Seth had consented to his work demand but commanded that he not tire himself out too much, as he had decided where they would go for the dinner he'd promised before his trip.

He showered, then headed into his closet to figure out what he should wear. Seth always looked so perfect. However, he didn't have to look long. A long garment bag hung inside, prominently displayed, with a note attached.

For this evening, pet.

S

He carefully brought it to the bed where he could check out what was inside. Soft, slate gray dress slacks and a deep indigo silk shirt. There were even socks and a belt to match in the bottom of the bag.

He struggled with the idea of Seth giving him things, not because of the difference in social status between them, but because he did not want Seth to see him as a charity case. But the clothes were hot, and he knew Seth would be pleased if he wore them. James still worried about his use of the word *submissive*, scared that Seth was going to turn into someone he was unable to be with, but he couldn't bring himself to back away either.

Once dressed, he waited in the great room for Seth to arrive. He tried to read, but had given up after reading the same page about three times with no idea what it had said. T.V.? No point. Television never held his attention to begin with. He only had the blasted thing for when he needed to follow the news or weather, though he usually used his laptop or cell. He was about to grab a sketchbook when he heard a car pull up outside. He got up and hurried to the door. He knew Seth walked faster than he could, and didn't want to make him wait.

Opening the door, he was met with Seth dressed almost identically, but for him it seemed oddly casual. The burgundy top made his eyes seem even more vivid than usual. His lips quirked with a smile as he reached out and wrapped his warm arms around James's waist. "Are you going to just stand there and stare at me, or are you ready to go?"

"No, I'm ready," James said. *As ready as I'm ever going to be.*

"Good. First, we eat then we will head over to Britt's gallery. She called and asked to see you." Seth led him to the Audi A7 he had seen once before, and held the door open for him. James had started to reach for the handle, but Seth's rigid body and stern demeanor let him know that *he* would tend to the door. He opened the door and left James with no option but to sit, which he did.

Once Seth was seated and buckled in, James cleared his throat and spoke. "You do know I can open doors and such myself, right? I'm really not an invalid."

"It has nothing to do with your ability to do such things, James. It is my pleasure to care for you, and it is yours to allow yourself to be cared for and protected. I explained this to you before, baby. Now, your only job tonight it to have fun with me." Seth seemed so calm and sure of himself that it was hard to disagree with him.

"Seth?" James asked quietly, unsure how to ask what he needed. Afraid to hear the possible answer even more.

"Yes, pet."

"You do realize I'm not a girl, a poodle, or a cripple, right? Please don't be angry, but—"

With a laugh, Seth cut him off. "A poodle? Really? No, James, I do not think you are any of those things. Nor do I see you as a punching bag or as mindless decoration. I don't know what you are used to, other than your one ex." Seth paused, seemingly to rein in his anger, before he continued. "Did your parents never teach you how to be a gentleman? I see you do for others but oddly, you seem to take the same respect given as an insult. Why?"

The "why" was asked as if it was a question, but he knew it was actually a demand. A demand that went straight to his cock. Shifting in his seat, he tried to ignore the command, doubtful of Seth's ability to understand.

"James, I dislike repeating myself. Please answer the question," Seth insisted, his voice a combination of steel and honey.

"A proper gentleman holds the door for a woman, the elderly, or a child to show respect and to assist as they are weaker and need more care than a man," James quoted as if reading off a card.

Seth jerked beside him. Glancing at James, he continued to the restaurant. "Yes and no, baby. It's an act of common courtesy and respect, not one of degradation. As for being weaker, when you meet my mother, I would suggest you *never* suggest she is weak because she is a woman, not if you plan to keep all your parts in working order."

"Oh," James mumbled. He had never dated much. Victor had been his second boyfriend, and as bad as he was, he wanted to think of his first even less. Other than that, all he had to go on was his mother and her insistence that such things were degrading to women.

"It's about natural reciprocity, James. We each do things for the other that makes life better. We haven't discussed rules or limits yet, though I suppose that is a lapse in my judgment."

"I didn't mean to make you unhappy, Seth. I guess I'm just not used to how you do things," he explained quietly.

"Then let me make this part easy for you. I expect you to enjoy yourself when you are with me, and that includes allowing me the pleasure of caring for you. When out to dinner or something similar, that will include me opening doors and ordering for you as I did the first time I took you out. Can you handle that?"

"Yes. It will take some getting used to, but I appreciate that you want to care for me." It still felt weird to him, but with how Seth had explained everything, it seemed rude and ungrateful to not agree.

Before long, they pulled up to a small Indian restaurant, where Seth proceeded to come around and open his door again, and waited for him to stand before closing the door.

James felt a strong hand rest lightly on the small of his back when they entered the restaurant. It felt comfortable, like how holding hands had once seemed to him.

Once seated, Seth looked him over again. "Is there anything you do not like? While I expect you to abide by our discussion in the car, I do not wish to order you something you either don't want or cannot have."

"I prefer the seafood or vegetarian dishes and only up to about a five or six on the heat. Thank you," he answered. He watched as his date—it felt odd thinking of being out on a date—then looked over the menu for a few minutes. He was glad for the lull in conversation and attention, though he didn't actually believe Seth was not always aware of what was happening around him.

He had been a young boy the last time someone had ordered for him, well, except for times like when he was in the hospital, of course. The only time people usually held doors for him was always accompanied by words or looks that made him feel like less of a man. Seth didn't make him feel that way. He knew Chase and a few of his friends would balk at the way Seth took over, like with the clothing, but he kind of liked that he didn't have to worry about if Seth would like this or that.

Their order taken, Seth returned his attention to James. "What has you so focused?" he asked gently.

"Just lost in thought."

"James, I know that look already. Your hands keep twitching, so share," Seth corrected.

"You'll think it's stupid," he explained. At the arched brow and slight frown, James quickly spoke again. "I was just thinking how I kind of liked not having to make the decisions. And, um, that made me think of when I was little and how my Pops, my dad's dad, always did things like order for Gram and hold her door, which led to me designing in my head. It's just, well, it's just how my mind jumps. I wasn't ignoring you, I swear."

He couldn't help how his mind worked or what would inspire him, though he often wished he could. He hadn't meant to zone out on Seth.

"Calm down, baby," Seth soothed. "I love watching you design, almost as much as watching you sleep. In both cases, I get to see the real you, not the one you present to the world. Would you like your bag brought in, so you can sketch while we wait? I won't mind."

James couldn't believe that Seth really meant it, that it was okay with him to let his muse take over when he should be focusing on him. "It... it's okay, Seth. I'll pay better attention."

"Obviously not or you would have said, 'Yes', with or without sir attached," he said, obviously teasing James. Without another word he stood, setting his napkin beside his spot, and excused himself. James watched Seth head back out the front door, a little confused as he hadn't brought his backpack with him. *Where's he going?* he wondered.

Feeling eyes on him, James looked up. He had assumed it was Seth returning, but the eyes that met his were a hard, sparking green.

Eyes he hadn't seen since, well, he didn't want to remember the last time he had been near Tyler.

He swallowed, hoping to keep the automatic tremble out of his voice. "H-hi, Tyler. Wh-what are you doing here?" *Go away, go away, go away, please,* he internally begged.

"I'm in town for the week, training conference. Funny running into you here," Tyler said, sitting down in Seth's chair. "And here I thought I'd be bored."

"Ty, please. That's Seth's seat you're in." After clearing his throat, he tried to speak louder. "You need to get up before he returns, Tyler."

Ignoring him, as he always had, the other ghost from his past gave him a grin. It was probably supposed to be charming; instead it made James cringe slightly and wish he were anywhere but there. "Guy can't bother to stay, he must not be overly interested. Not that I can blame him. You never were good for much, well, outside the bedroom anyway.

"Speaking of which, come on. Your lips can keep me company for a while," Tyler continued as he grabbed James's wrist, digging the bracelet that went to his silver thumb ring into his flesh. It was the same wrist Victor had kicked and stomped. A cry slipped out as the pain shot up his arm when Tyler twisted slightly.

Suddenly, Seth was there, hand over Tyler's, stopping him mid-twist.

"Let go of him," Seth snapped, his voice colder than James had ever heard before. He could feel Tyler try to twist free, but Seth didn't let go.

"Whatever, man. Lousy piece of ass anyway," Tyler said, and finally released his vise grip on James's arm.

The next few minutes passed in a hollow blur. He knew Seth had Tyler removed, he heard that much, but he couldn't seem to focus. His two worst nightmares had come back to haunt him. Maybe his little brother could show up and make his hell complete.

"James." Seth's voice intruded on his internal freak-out. "Come on, we're leaving." He then noticed Seth had a to-go bag in one hand and his crutches in the other. Numbly, he got to his feet and followed Seth back out to the car.

"COME on, baby. We're going up to my place," Seth murmured as he gently caressed James's cheek. It was only when touched that he noticed they were stopped, well, parked more specifically, at some fancy condo.

chapter seven

"MEL, I'm telling you that this is beyond just him having a couple of bullies for exes. Once I made his ex, Tyler, release his bruising grip on James, he didn't speak again until I demanded he respond once we were in my condo," Seth explained as he paced the floor in Mel's office, a tumbler of whiskey in his hand. The previous night had been a long one, filled with painful stories from James's past, a pain that Seth wasn't sure he could fix. "And once he did start, he spent most of the time talking, in tears curled up against my chest. He's terrified I will judge him because of his past, a past he didn't choose. I don't know what to do."

"Well, that's a first. The great and powerful Seth Burns at a loss for what to do…. Never thought I'd live to see the day," Mel chided.

"Don't," Seth snapped. He stopped long enough to glower at his best friend since college before resuming his attempt to wear a path in the floor. Though there was a large age difference, thanks to Seth starting college at fifteen, they had become fast friends and would do anything for each other. "You know how brittle some creative types are, Mel. James was abused, used, raped, and even when he escaped he just ended up in the hands of the ass that landed him in the hospital. I didn't manage to get the story of Victor out of him. I've never seen that level of pain and fear before."

"Sorry, man," Mel replied. Leaning forward to brace his forearms on his knees, he looked Seth over and frowned. "Is he really worth all this energy and worry? You don't usually get so attached, especially so quickly."

Seth knew what he was usually like, *thank you very much*. He knew he did not usually get overly attached to his relationships, but James was different. For the first time in longer than he wanted to contemplate, he wanted to keep a partner, and not just for a short while. He wasn't sure how it happened, especially with how short a time they had known each other, but he felt his heart was no longer fully his own. After the revelation, he'd waited for fear and worry to consume him, but it never manifested. What had appeared was longing and concern.

"Ha. He doesn't believe that he is worth the energy and worry, but I do. I have never been so drawn to anyone." Seth knew he probably sounded like one of Mel's teenaged daughters mooning over some boy, but there was something about James that called to him in a way he couldn't resist and did not want to, honestly.

"What about his family? Maybe one of them could help you find a way past James's fears," Mel replied with a shrug.

"His little brother is best friends, still, with the psycho, Tyler. James said he told his mother what happened back then and instead of helping him she condemned him for being a pervert and wanting to have sex with a man. His brother went so far as to claim that he lied because his buddy spurned James's advances.

"He never spoke of his father, though I know he's still alive and with his mom. I'm wondering about their relationship or lack thereof, considering."

"Hey, man. Don't give up yet. You remember how hard it was with Britt? But with your help, I managed to get past her fears and look how happy we've been since! We have three beautiful children and we are still very much together and in love. If your James is really this important and special to you, you'll find a way and I'll back you, you know that."

Seth understood what Mel was saying, especially considering what he went through to win Britt. She hadn't gone through the same things, but still, she had been afraid to open up and get involved with Mel when they met. Even back then, he had been good at figuring people out. He just needed to find the key to his pet; that was all.

JAMES had been nervous since Seth had mentioned two days prior they needed to visit her, but then Tyler had made his agonizing appearance and thrown everything out of form and sequence. God, he hated that man, not that Ty had ever cared what he thought or felt. They were headed for a meeting at Britt's gallery.

Once Seth parked the car, he went around the front and opened the door politely, extending a hand to offer assistance if James needed. The pavement shimmered from the rain that had only stopped falling about ten minutes prior to Seth's arrival. He still felt a little weird about the whole door thing, but he couldn't deny that it also gave him a little thrill and made him feel like maybe he was something special to Seth. He hoped he was. He stood and got settled with his forearm crutches, then leaned enough to bump his shoulder to Seth's. Again, he wondered why they were here and about Seth's persistent silence since he'd picked him up from his cottage. He didn't seem upset or angry, he just seemed lost in thought.

"Seth, back up a little, please. You're too close and I can see the oil sheen on the surface here. I would really rather not land on my ass tonight. Besides, I'm sure you can think of better uses for it than that," he teased with a wink. He wanted to get some kind of reaction from his slightly withdrawn lover.

"Ha, ha, ha. Sorry about that, baby. I'm still learning the range you need. And yes, I can think of much better ways to treat that sexy backside of yours," Seth said and patted the backside in question, then backed up a little.

"Come on, Britt is expecting you. Actually, she has a few people she wants you to meet so put on your happy face and let's go."

"People?" *What does he mean* people?

Seth cupped his cheek, brushed it with his thumb. Leaning in, he kissed James softly, with just enough pressure to ignite a flame but not enough to consume either of them. "Take a deep breath, pet. She had a request from someone who wants to purchase one of the paintings you contracted with her to sell. He wants to meet the artist, and considering the amount he's paying, she consented to call and arrange a meeting. She didn't tell me who the buyer is but the more exposure you get, the better your salability."

"Not to sound rude or ungrateful, but why tell you instead of me if it's my meeting?"

"Timing. I stopped by to see her and Mel and she mentioned it. Plus, you have been so stressed the last few days; I thought a surprise would be welcome."

"Thank you, I think," James mumbled and continued inside, Seth opening the gallery door for him, of course. Once inside, James looked around for Brittany Holcomb. Her voice found him before he saw her.

"James," she chirped. "Wonderful to see you again. I have someone I want to introduce you to, though Seth knows him already."

"Oh, okay. Lead the way."

"I do?" Seth asked. He seemed puzzled, which was an odd look for him in James's opinion.

"Well, you ought to know me, hun" came a strong yet lilting voice. James turned to see the owner of said voice and was surprised to see a short, rather pretty man step around Brittany. He was about five-six or so, light caramel-colored skin, with dark black hair that was streaked a vibrant cherry red. He had delicate, almost fey-like features and a huge smile.

"Zach? You're the mystery buyer Britt's been raving about?" Seth asked as the small, excitable man hugged him.

With a bright smile and a wink, Zach turned to face James. "Zachariah Summer Macey, at your service, Mr. Bryant. Everyone calls me Zach. Britt, isn't she a sweetie, says you're the artist of the work I want to buy. I'm hoping she's right 'cuz I also want to commission some work both for the hotels Seth's company is building and for a couple of other clients as well.

"Oh, have you told him about the hotels yet, Seth? I just saw the marketing designs and branding and I just love it!"

James was stunned and not completely sure how to respond when his internal confusion was disrupted by Seth's booming laugh.

"Zachy, dear, take a deep breath. Seriously, you need to do your research before you go opening that little mouth of yours," Seth teased him. James felt a sudden pang at their playful banter. Was this one of Seth's previous lovers?

With an adorable pout Zach looked at Seth and grumped, "What? You're the one who decided to personally oversee the start of the project after that Neanderthal, Mark, botched the original design. What'd I say? I told you not to hire that loudmouthed—"

"Zach," Seth interrupted. "Quiet for a minute, please. James is the artist that designed the branding you just squealed about to him."

"And he's the artist you requested to meet and you just bought three of his paintings," Brittany added with a little giggle.

"Um, if I'm the artist he wants to meet then shouldn't I get to say hello at some point?" James asked, struggling not to laugh too hard. He didn't want to offend the bouncy little man, but it was too funny.

"Yes," Zach said, shooing the others away with a wave of his hands. "I'm here to meet the delicious artist boy here, not to be picked on by you two corporate-drone types."

Seth seemed to sober when Zach said delicious, making James wonder again, why. "Zach," Seth snapped. His tone turned to that powerful, commanding one that so excited James, even though he disliked his own reaction to it.

"Seth," James murmured and gently touched Seth's arm. "He was just teasing, not coming on to me. Relax, please."

"Sorry, pet. I'll go speak with Britt while you and Zach talk." He then turned and offered his arm to Brittany, and they left the two of them alone.

"I didn't mean to upset the big man," Zach mumbled as he watched the two leave. "But, I should have known better than to tease you like that. He's always too territorial with his pets," he added with a sigh. "Any who…. You're amazing, man! I just bought three of your paintings and I want to commission a few more, though it's a little weird that you're also the graphic designer that did the branding and all. Huh. Britt should have told me. Oh well. Look, Jay. Can I call you Jay? Right. Look, you're not the only artist I've picked, but your art is so passionate and raw; I want more of your stuff. Since Seth didn't know it was me who wanted to meet you, he didn't tell you who I am. I'm on retainer with him and a few other corporations for interior design. Oh, here," Zach continued, completely overwhelming James in the process. He quickly whipped out a bright pink business card, then continued rambling. "I'll also need to know about prints versus the original artwork for display, sizes you are comfortable working with, oh, and mediums. I know you do fabu oils and Britt says your oils and acrylic mixed work is just as delish, but…."

As their discussion wound down, Zach threw him again. "Now that that's all settled, you just have to tell me about you and Seth. I've been looking but I don't see any bindings on you or even any normal marks. He called you *pet*, so I'm assuming you two are together, right?"

Trying to process everything the man said, he was suddenly very nervous. They seemed to know each other well, so what did Zach mean about binding and marks? "How do you mean, Zach?" he asked, his voice cracked partway through.

"You know, you're not wearing a collar, cuffs, or anything I can see. Your one wrist is a little bruised, but since there isn't a matching one, that doesn't make sense," Zach explained excitedly.

"Why would I have any of those things, much less because of Seth? He's been very sweet and kind to me since we met." James couldn't control the rolling in his stomach at the words and images going through his mind. Was there something about Seth he needed to know, to run from?

James heard the door creak open more but was too focused on what Zack was saying to care who it might be.

"Pets are marked, silly. Wow, you must be really new if you don't know that. Never mind," Zach said, waving away the last bit of conversation.

Before he could continue talking, Seth was beside James, his hand on James's lower back. Holding up his hand to Zach in a shushing motion, he leaned in and murmured softly, "Shhh, baby. Calm down."

James tried to focus and calm but all he could think of was why Zach thought he should have bruises. He wanted to leave, *now*, but knew he didn't have a chance of out maneuvering Seth. He also knew he trembled slightly but was doing his best to hide his fears.

"Zach, I would appreciate you sticking to work-related topics with James. You are completely out of line, and you know it," Seth demanded. Zach seemed to shrink a little at both the words and tone Seth had used. "Just because you enjoy pain does not mean everyone does. Now, are you two finished with everything?"

Brittany took Zach off to finish their part of the transaction— the work was being commissioned through her gallery after all—and Seth led James to a small office area. Once seated, Seth took James's hand and played with his fingers gently, careful of the silver ring splints, while he waited for James to speak. He had learned that pushing too hard was the opposite of helpful if he wanted James to talk. After a few interminably long minutes, James spoke, though he didn't look up and his voice was soft. "Why would your, um, friend think I should have a collar or bruises? He's one of your exes, isn't he? You did those things with him?"

Taking a deep breath, James blinked, trying to keep back the tears that threatened to fall. He quickly took out his cell and sent the rescue message Chase had programmed into his cell ages ago, only adding "@ gallery" to the end. He didn't let Seth see the text.

Seth quirked a brow at James's cell but said nothing. Slowly, he extended his right hand to caress James's cheek before using his fingers to carefully lift James's face up. His gentle confidence showed in both his voice and motions. "Yes. Zach and I were involved many years ago, but it was more friends with benefits than a true relationship. You have no need to fear your place with me, baby.

"As to the collar and bruises, I do tend to gift my partners with tokens that show who they are with, but Zach is much more into the public BDSM world than I ever was and sees the tokens as required. You have no need to worry about the bruises he mentioned. Zach's a pain slut, and proudly so, but he tends to see others from his own point of view. I will never cause you harm, not that he saw his bruises as harm."

"I don't understand, Seth. Why would you hurt him? How long before you decide to hurt me too? I can't allow that again, you know that. You swore I was safe with you!"

"You are safe, baby, but here is not really the place to have in-depth discussions of sexual practices and flavors of various people." Placing a calming hand on his lower back, Seth met his eyes and smiled gently. "I will speak with Britt and Zach and then we can leave. I promise to answer any questions you have once we are settled." Seth then bent to kiss James's forehead before leaving him in the private office.

James waited, hoping Chase would be quick. He knew he would have to eventually talk to Seth about all of this, but he needed time to decide how to deal with what he had learned. Seth was violent, sexually, with a previous lover and obviously had no remorse for his actions. How could he trust Seth not to turn on him eventually? The term pet had already bothered him some, but in context with the term collar, it added a whole new level of nerves and fear. He'd gone through the whole thing of Victor thinking he owned him—he never wanted to deal with that again.

Just as he began to panic that Seth would return and want to leave, a new text popped up. Chase was outside, waiting. James quickly got himself together and headed toward the doors, hoping to meet Chase before the others came back for him.

Once he was in Chase's car, he sent Seth a text. » I need time. Sorry. «

"I'm assuming that since you had me pick you up and that Seth didn't follow you out, that you need away from him for some reason. So, your place or mine?" Chase asked lightly. James knew his best friend wouldn't push for more information yet. One of his more endearing qualities, really.

"I'll explain later but yours, please. Seth will try going to mine, I'm sure. I just need space and time right now. Thanks, Chase. You're my hero," he added with as much camp as he could muster.

By the time they reached Chase's apartment, Seth had tried to call and had sent texts in an attempt to get James to talk to him. James was tempted, but ended up resending his original text, then turned off his phone for the night.

chapter eight

SETH had called and sent texts, to no avail, after James left the gallery with Chase. Though watching taillights disappear was no comfort to him, he had seen who picked James up, thankfully, or he would have gone out of his mind with worry. About two and a half hours later, his phone chirped with a new text message.

»This is Chase. I managed to sneak James's cell long enough to get your #. Hope it's ok. We need to talk. Don't call, just type.«

Seth read the message over, wondering why Chase was contacting him like this, but was hopeful that maybe Chase might be the key to getting through to his antsy lover.

»Hello, Chase. James ok?«

»Upset but ok. He's sleeping right now. What happened that got him so freaked?«

»This conversation would be best in person. Voice at least. Meet me?«

»James will be pissed if he wakes up.«

»Leave a note that you ran out for a few minutes. We need to talk.«

»IDK…«

»For James?«

»Fine. Meet me @ The Buzz in 30«

»Agreed. Thank you.«

Seth quickly grabbed his keys and wallet from the table where he had thrown them down when he came in. He had been so upset he'd nearly thrown them across the room. He was even less certain that he could overcome James's past so they could have a future together after what happened earlier that evening. *Damn Zach! Damn Victor! And damn, to the lowest pits of Hades, Tyler!*

"DON'T *mistake his fear and such for weakness. Or his lack of family as a lack of support.*" Of all the things Chase had said during their "conference," that was the part that kept replaying the most, especially late at night while he was failing miserably to sleep. How could James's own family have subjected him to so much? How could he help James past the pain and fear so they could truly explore more together? Seth wanted so much more than just James's body, delicious though it was. He wanted James's heart and soul too.

It had taken Seth, working with Chase, a full three weeks to break down enough of the wall James had erected between them before he would agree to see him again. It had been an insanely long three weeks. Tonight, James had agreed to have dinner with him again, but the conditions grated on his nerves. They were to have dinner at Chase's apartment. James was cooking, though he had no idea what, and Chase would be there as a layer of protection for James. Or, that's how James probably saw it. James still didn't know about Chase meeting him or all the texting and calls that had happened over the last few weeks.

Seth sat in his Audi A7, looking toward the front of Chase's apartment building. He needed to pull himself together, now. He knew that, but his nerves didn't want to listen. Taking a few slow, deep breaths, Seth got himself under control and exited the car. Unlike the first time, he had a single silver rose carefully clutched in his fingers. He always tried to be romantic, but the last few weeks had worn him thin, especially when the first few gifts he had sent to James had been returned.

Seth was mildly disappointed but not surprised when it was Chase, not James, who answered the door to the small apartment. "Come in, Seth. James is in the kitchen," he explained. He leaned in and dropped his voice to barely a whisper and added, "And I don't care if you like what he's making or not, you will love it. He's so nervous I'm surprised he's kept anything down all day. Go easy on our boy, please."

Seth smiled at the protectiveness, glad his love had such a caring and true friend. "If he made it, it will be exactly what I need and want. And Chase, thank you."

Taking Seth's coat, he led him to the open kitchen area. The apartment wasn't a studio, but it did have a rather open layout where the kitchen flowed into the dining and living areas.

"Jamie dear, your date is here," Chase sing-songed, a huge cheeky grin plastered on his face.

James sat on a tall stool that had rolling coasters on the bottom, allowing him easier and assisted movement without requiring the use of his hands like his forearm crutches. Seth had noticed a similar stool in James's kitchen before, but hadn't thought much about it at the time. *Creative solution.* The apartment was filled with the most delicious scents!

"Hello, Seth," James said softly as he accepted the single rose. Seth could tell he was nervous, but he was pleasantly surprised by the open longing written on James's face as their eyes met. Looking down, James bit his bottom lip before he continued, "Um, dinner is almost ready. Chase set the table already, but I can get you something to drink while we wait. If, um, if you'd like. I have wine, beer, juice, soda, or water."

He could tell James was nervous even without the lip nibbling or the slight babble, but he was so pleased to just be there he honestly didn't care. "I can get the drinks, James. You don't have to do everything yourself."

"I know, Seth, but...."

"But you are all worked up and don't know what to do with all the extra energy? Fine, pet. I will have a glass of whatever wine you picked out to go with dinner. I would like you to have one as well," he replied as he sat at the counter so he could watch James work. He loved to watch James, whether cooking, sleeping, painting, in the throes of passion, or well, simply doing nothing.

He was still at a loss as to how this sweet, sexy, unassuming man had gotten past all his carefully constructed barriers and stolen his heart. It killed him that he couldn't be honest and tell James how deeply he felt already, but he knew that would send James running again. James was not ready for that yet, he was certain, but it didn't change how he felt or what he wanted. Now to get James past his fears.

The small smile that graced James's face as he set Seth's wine glass down in front of him made Seth's heart ache and his pulse race a little more. He knew James had no idea how beautiful a man he was, but he wondered at his luck to have found him before someone else who would cherish him as he deserved snapped him up.

"Thank you, James," Seth said softly. Their fingers had barely touched as he had taken the glass, but that simple touch had been enough to tent his slacks and dry his mouth. He only wished those fingers weren't marred by the silver rings still; he hated that he couldn't take away the damage James's ex had caused. He liked the look, just hated the reason.

"Well boys," Chase interrupted. "Why don't we start on the salad and then move on? You two can moon over each other while we eat."

"Chase," James snapped. "No being an ass just because you have one."

Batting his eyes, feigning innocence, Chase asked, "What, you don't like my ass?"

James pinched the bridge of his nose as he closed his eyes and shook his head. "Chase, so help me. Love you dearly, though I do, I will beat you if you don't behave. Now, grab the bread and knife while I get the salads."

James looked up at Seth with a shy smile. "Would you care to join us, Seth?"

Seth watched as James insisted on setting the salad plates he had prepared at each setting. Once he felt it was safe to interrupt, he gently guided James to the place he indicated, pulled out his chair, and waited until James was settled before he took his own seat.

"This looks wonderful, James. Did you make all this yourself?" Seth asked, gesturing with one hand toward the salads, fresh baked bread, and assorted additions and toppings laid out. He knew his lover could cook, but just the scent alone made him want to salivate and gnaw on something.

James blushed but said, "Fresh asparagus salad, honey wheat bread, and the main course, yes. Chase made the turtle cheesecake for dessert, though. I was never any good at baking."

"You do fine, Jamie. Your mom was just jealous at how good a cook you were, that's all," Chase countered forcefully. He turned to Seth and added playfully, "I have yet to try anything he cooks and not want to devour it whole. Now children, eat up so I can."

While they ate their salads, the three men chatted about work, James's art, and the hotel, but it all stayed very light. Seth wanted to push into why he had been without his lover for three weeks, but knew he had to be patient, or at least pretend to be.

Chase sashayed into the kitchen and messed with dishes and food once the salads were done. It seemed that Chase was to serve the main meal, a fact Seth was pleased to see. James often tried to do too much and wound up putting himself through far more pain than was necessary.

When Chase served the main course, it impressed and surprised Seth. Beef tips in a portobello mushroom sauce over a bed of sautéed red and yellow bell peppers and red onion. There was a salt-crusted baked potato with steamed broccoli and glazed baby carrots on the side.

Without looking, James grabbed the A1 that was on the table and handed it over to Chase. Chase did the same with the pepper grinder, handing it to James. Seth sat back and watched the interactions of the two best friends, amused yet mildly jealous of their connection.

James stopped and looked up at Seth suddenly, his fork partway to his lips. "Seth, is there something wrong with the food?" It killed Seth to see how tense he suddenly became.

"No, baby. The food looks wonderful and smells even better." He took a thoughtful bite of the tips with a pepper and gravy. "Ooh, and tastes… divine."

James beamed at the compliment, seemingly pleased over a simple fact. "I'm glad you like it. I couldn't decide what to make for you. It was actually Chase's idea."

"James, look at me," Seth softly commanded. It took a moment, but James finally did as instructed. "No matter what you had chosen, as long as it was from your heart, I would have loved it. This is a gift you have given me, and as with all gifts from you, I will enjoy. Never fear that I will not appreciate or cherish what you choose to share with or give to me. No matter what form it takes."

James seemed unable to respond, and Seth watched with great satisfaction as a lovely pink flush spread across James's features. Even the tips of his perfect ears were pink.

The conversation went back to being more casual while they dug in and enjoyed the wonderful meal James made. Part way through, Chase cleared his throat and asked a question he was sure James had wanted to ask. "Seth, I wanted to ask something and hope you won't be offended, but why do you call James 'pet'? You said you weren't really into the BDSM scene like your friend but…."

Seth paused, thinking how to answer. "Well, yes and no, if I understand your truncated question, Chase. My mother will call my brother and me pet 'til the day she passes. My father's the same. They both use the term with others that they are close to, even some of my friends. Mom even calls Mel pet, if you can imagine. Our dog, Cindy, was not even a pet if you asked my mother. Cindy was my poor, slightly misshapen sister. I grew up with it being used as an endearment."

"Seth," James interrupted, though he could see a softening as his explanation worked its way past James's walls. "I know there's more to it than that. As Chase and Zach Macey mentioned, you are into *that* too, at least somewhat."

"I could happily throttle Zach for what he said to you as he led you to believe something that was mostly untrue about me. Yes, pet is also used in the way you seem to be pushing about, but while I have referred to you as 'my pet' it was never meant in a demeaning manner.

"Let me ask you something and maybe that will help you understand my point of view better. If we are dating and we go to a restaurant or club and some man, some boy, tries to hit on me, grab me or something like that, would that be okay with you? Would you be upset that that person touched your boyfriend, lover, whatever term you want to use?"

James seemed to think for a few moments before he looked back up, a slightly haunted look in his eyes. "I wouldn't like that. If you were with me then the hypothetical guy should respect that there is already a claim on you, though I—"

"Seth, James would never try to stop you if you reacted or accepted the other man's attention. You need to understand that," Chase explained when James's words died in his throat.

With a slight nod to Chase, Seth continued. "You would have every right to be upset, baby. If we are together—and as I told you before, I don't share—then you should see me as yours. Not a possession to harm or control in a negative fashion, but as a partner that you cherish and can count on.

"Yes, you are my pet. My pet because I see us as having a relationship. My pet, my cherished one, my beloved. Hell, even if I did see you as something to truly own, being that kind of pet would get you pampered, played with, cared for, and shown off. Is any of that really bad?" Seth asked, brow arched as he awaited James's reaction.

"I—I don't want to be with someone that would show me off, want to share me, make me do things for others, or that would hurt me, Seth. I do care for you, but I can't be that person. Please understand that," James pleaded. Seth could tell he was scared, but he was determined to get him past it. Past in the past, so they could have a future.

"James, have I tolerated anyone harming you, even if I wasn't there? Have I allowed anyone to touch you that shouldn't? That you didn't want to touch you?"

"No," James squeaked. Trying to control his voice, he tried again. "No, you haven't. But what Zach said, you showed no remorse for hurting him within your relationship with him. You even called him a slut. Is that the kind of attitude I have to look forward to if I continue to see you?" he asked so earnestly it nearly broke Seth. Had no one ever truly loved and cared for James, other than Chase?

"James, I said he was a pain slut. I also said he was proud of being said slut. He's actually very set about not being shared. He would never even scene with someone that tried that. He is a one-on-one-only guy. A pain slut is someone that gets off on pain. Well, to them the pain becomes pleasure and they can be a bit extreme about it. Most people get a little pleasure out of pain, but for someone like Zach, it's a necessary part of sex.

"I will not apologize for the pain I caused Zach all those years ago, and he would be mortified if I ever did. I gave him what he asked for. And before you say it, I mean that literally, not an assumption to justify my actions."

Seth caught James's skeptical look and decided to try a different approach. "You know what he bought me right after we got together the first time?" Seth asked, not sure Zach would appreciate him sharing this but well, he should have kept his damn mouth shut to begin with.

"No," James whispered.

Seth noticed Chase watching the conversation from his place. He kept quiet, *thankfully*, Seth thought.

"He showed up at my apartment with a rattan cane, wrapped up. It even had a big purple bow on it, if you can believe that. I actually went through training so I could use the toys he wanted me to use without causing him actual damage."

Seth watched as a look of absolute horror spread across the features of the man he had quickly come to love and cherish. He could tell immediately that James was not listening to the point he was trying to make. James's next words confirmed as much. "Someone taught you how to beat your lover?"

"No, someone helped train me in how to bring my now ex-lover the pleasure he preferred. His extreme need of pain-pleasure is what actually split us up. Well, that and the fact that neither of us was in love with the other.

"Think about it, James. Did Zach seem afraid of me? Worried for you? Did he shake or lose his color?" Seth asked, knowing that if James would just think about this objectively, then he would understand and not be so worried.

"Well, no. He seemed put out that I didn't have bruises or a collar, though," James countered, looking more uncertain of his viewpoint, or so Seth hoped.

"Baby, he was disappointed for you, not upset or afraid. He's a romantic at heart. Every time he even thinks I'm interested in someone, he goes all gushy—yes, that's a word. His word in fact—hoping that this time I'll have found my life partner. It means he liked you and was hoping that we were more than a fling. It's why he is so upset he scared you."

"Really?" James asked, his eyes wide with unashamed pleading. He desperately wanted everything Seth had said to be true. If it was, then he didn't need to be afraid Seth would change and hurt him. He admitted to being dominant but also to not enjoying the sensual and sexual violence that James feared. *Please, please, please be true,* James's heart begged.

chapter nine

AFTER two more supervised dates, James decided he was being stupid about Seth and allowed things to go back to the way they were before. Early the next week, Seth came over to watch movies and spend time with James, though James secretly hoped to resume their more physical relationship soon as well.

James decided to pause the movie they had agreed upon long enough to get another drink. He turned to ask if Seth wanted another drink when Seth framed his face with his hands, leaned in, and gently kissed him. James grasped the back of the couch to keep his balance as he quickly lost himself in the warm, demanding yet sweet power of Seth's mouth on his. He realized a whimper had escaped him as he gave in and moved to straddle Seth's lap and deepen the kiss.

He settled his hands atop Seth's shoulders before sliding one down his chest. His ring-braces caught slightly on the soft material of the undershirt before he slid it around Seth's waist to hug him close. James pulled back to break the kiss long enough to pull off his own shirt and toss it behind him, not caring where it landed.

After swooping in to steal another firm but gentle kiss, James leaned back again and divested Seth of his shirt before he pressed his now bare chest to Seth's. He let out a long sigh, too caught up in sensation and longing for Seth to do more than moan as he nuzzled his face into the crook of Seth's neck.

One of Seth's hands moved from James's face to tenderly take possession of the back of his neck, tilting his head as he threaded his fingers into James's hair. When Seth tugged lightly on his hair, James nearly lost it, suddenly craving more of Seth's control and passion.

"Baby," Seth murmured against James's lips. He was rewarded for his tug by James's deep, throaty moan.

With a low growl, Seth pulled James tighter against him. James shifted again and they both gasped as James rocked, their groins aligned and pressed together despite the now irritating layers of clothes between them. As Seth took complete control of the now ravishing kiss, James ground harder against Seth.

James let out a wail when Seth grasped his hips and forced them to still. "Not yet, pet. Let me up," Seth gently commanded.

"But," James pouted; it was nearly a whine. He didn't want to stop. He wanted Seth, damn it!

"Let me up, baby. I promise you will like this," Seth countered.

Once he was up, he pulled James back into his arms for another soul-searing kiss before he slid his hands down and cupped James's firm ass and demanded that James wrap his arms and legs around him. He carried James to the large oak bed and carefully settled him there before quickly divesting them of the rest of their clothing.

James watched as Seth grabbed a silk scarf that was folded into his pocket. He tossed it up by the pillows before setting his knee on the edge of the bed and then carefully crawled up the bed and his lover.

He began his assault with kisses to the tender skin of James's thighs, ascending the body slowly as he kissed up his thighs to the prominent hip bones, followed the light trail of hair from his groin up to his belly button, up to gently lap and kiss each nipple in turn. The entire way up, Seth deliberately, it seemed, missed all contact with James's throbbing cock, which was leaking steadily against his lower abdomen. James squirmed but couldn't get any friction, no matter how he moved.

"Seth," James snapped. "Please."

Seth continued his assault on James's senses and body.

"Arms above your head, baby," Seth whispered, pausing to trace James's ear with the tip of his tongue. "I want to do something different, but you have to trust me and do as instructed. No arguments."

James swallowed hard but was too far gone with desire and lust to stop now. He slowly raised his arms till they were nearly to the headboard. He started to panic when he noticed the scarf Seth had put there earlier but was distracted from his worries when Seth suddenly pressed his groin down, grinding into James enough to pull a deep groan from his lips.

A few moments later, James felt something being placed into his hands. "Take the ends in your hands. Nothing happens that you don't want, baby. As long as you keep a hold of the scarf, I will keep making love to your body, but if you let go, I stop. No questions, no hesitation. If you need me to stop, let go."

James couldn't find his voice so he simply nodded his agreement. He wasn't sure about being restrained by agreement, but he wanted, no needed, Seth so much he was willing to do almost anything right then to be with him.

"Good. Now, stretch out completely and let me have a little fun," Seth murmured against James's lips.

Seth's thumb brushed James's nipple as he dug in the drawer next to the bed, searching for the supplies he needed.

James writhed beneath him, every touch drawing out little mewling sounds. He tried to follow Seth's movements, but his eyes were glassy with lust and his brain only focused on pleasure and Seth.

Seth tossed the lube and condoms beside James and straddled him again. "Calm down, baby. I promise you'll like this."

James wanted to wrap his hands in Seth's hair and his legs around his waist, but he couldn't move his legs as he hung on for dear life to the silk that he had now wrapped around his hands, needing a better hold. He didn't want any of it to stop!

Seth kissed him again as he opened the lube. Whimpering, James watched Seth's every move.

"I want you to watch, but don't come. Just watch me." Seth then slicked his fingers and rose above James. He slowly slid two fingers into himself, a small smile tugging at his lips as his eyes closed briefly.

James couldn't help but raise his arms as if he would reach down to Seth, but the tug from the scarf reminded him that he couldn't touch. He had never wanted to touch anyone so badly as right then.

He was drowning in the heat as he watched Seth add another finger and stretch himself.

Seth moaned, working his fingers deeper, in and out of his body. James knew what he planned. Why else would he prepare his own body for penetration, but James couldn't make it fit within his experience. He didn't top. Ever.

Slowly, Seth withdrew his fingers with a moan. He grabbed the condom and quickly rolled it down James's beautiful cock, taking extra care to use plenty of lube and draw out the strokes a little before he crawled forward.

"Seth?" James whispered, barely able to force out enough breath to make himself heard.

"Shh, baby. Just let me love you." He positioned James's cock at his entrance and slowly pushed down, forcing his body to open and accept his lover within. Seth paused when James felt his head pop inside. Seth seemed determined to draw it out, to make this last.

Squirming, James gasped and wrapped the scarf around his hands, pulling his body taut beneath Seth's assault.

Sinking down, Seth leaned forward and braced himself on James's chest. He didn't move right away. Small tremors ran through James's body as he tried to be good for Seth. James moved underneath Seth in a sudden, sharp jolt, and begged, "Seth, please. I. God. Move!"

With a slight chuckle, Seth moved his hips so he slid up and down James, taking him all the way in and then pulling up until only the crown was still inside. He continued to move up and down, grinding when he hit bottom.

After a few long moments, James joined in, pistoning upward as Seth thrust himself down, to increase the power and pleasure to them both. Every couple of thrusts James realized his cock tapped Seth's prostate, as he would lose his breath or shout and after only a few hits, he was slamming down with such abandon that James was certain he would feel it for days. James would too, from the bruises caused by Seth's fingers and body slamming into his, not that either man cared.

Seth's cock leaked, and he could feel his orgasm building. From the strangled cries, it was obvious that James also struggled to not climax.

Seth sat up and grabbed his cock, only pumping twice before he cried out, coating James's stomach and chest with his come. He wasn't even done decorating his lover's body with his seed when James arched up, screamed, and came inside Seth.

As they collapsed together, Seth wrapped his body around James, and they drifted together on their orgasm high. Both utterly sated and complete—together.

Blinking, James smiled, and a sensual yet slightly confused look crossed his face as he finally seemed to focus on Seth.

Before he could speak, Seth bent up and nipped his bottom lip. "Don't let go yet, James. I'll be right back."

Seth then carefully shifted, and James's now spent cock slid out of his body. Seth removed the condom, then moved slowly over to the ensuite and returned with a warm, damp cloth to clean James; he had tended to his own mess already, James noticed. He tossed the cloth back toward the door, but chose to settle against James's side instead of climbing back on top.

"Let go, baby. I want to hold you," Seth murmured. He pulled James's arms down and helped him turn on his side.

"Seth?" James began.

"Yes."

James sighed and stretched before he replied. "Wow" was all he managed to say. He wanted to ask Seth why he'd done it, tell him how amazing he'd felt, or even tell him how much he loved him, but he was afraid to voice his thoughts—afraid that he wouldn't want to hear what Seth said in reply.

With a chuckle, Seth nuzzled into James's neck again, simply breathing in his shy lover. "Wow, indeed. You felt… amazing, pet." He shifted to rest his cheek against the top of James's head and closed his eyes.

"Rest, baby. We can talk about all the things rattling around in your head later. I'm not going anywhere."

James gave a satisfied sigh, snuggled into Seth's side a little tighter, and drifted off, thinking of nothing but how much he loved the man holding him and how he never wanted him to leave.

"WAKE up, baby. You're going to be late if you don't get up now," Seth said while he gently shook James.

"Mmm, don't wanna get up," James nearly whined. "Someone kept me up all night."

"Smart ass," Seth said with a chuckle. "Get up and eat your breakfast. We both need to get going."

Once James finally sat up, the sheet pooling sensually around his bare waist, Seth moved the tray across his lap. "You need to eat," Seth instructed. He leaned forward to place a gentle kiss on his lips before lifting a piece of melon to James's lips.

James pulled back slightly. "I can feed myself, Seth."

"I know that, now eat up, baby," Seth countered, again placing the melon to James's lips. With a put-upon sigh, James opened his mouth and accepted the sweet food. Seth stayed next to James and fed him until the plate was empty. Then they got up and ready for their respective days.

"Don't forget, I will pick you up at your office, James, and we can get lunch before the meeting at my office. Sandy is driving me crazy about getting you to possibly help with one of her other projects. I'm not sure what it is, but if you're not careful, we may just steal you away from that design firm you work for now."

With one last kiss, James and Seth headed to their cars and back to their work lives.

"JAMES, could you come here for a moment?" Carl Archer, James's senior manager, inquired shortly before lunch. He was standing in the hall near James's office.

"Sure, just a moment."

James quickly stood and once settled on his crutches, followed Carl out into the hallway. Seth stood next to Carl, decked out in one of his dark suits. He looked good enough to eat, James was sure of it. Or maybe just worship with his body for a few hours.

A slow smile spread across Seth's face as he took in James's surprise. "Hello, again."

"Um, hi, Mr. Burns," James replied. He was at work and Seth was a client, after all.

"James, Mr. Burns here was just telling me about how pleased he and Carrington Enterprises are with your work. He also mentioned that his buyer, Zach Macey, has purchased some of your work from one of the local galleries. Hell, I didn't even know you had any art in any of the galleries around here.

"Anyway, the point is that Seth wanted to make sure that his business and personal relationship with you, outside what he has employed us for, will not cause you any concerns at work. We do have rules about freelancing with current customers, but he has assured me that Mr. Macey's purchases were through the gallery and that neither he nor you realized the purchases were for Carrington until afterwards. Is this correct?" Carl asked. Though James could see he was not upset, he wondered about why they were discussing this out in the hall instead of in either of their offices.

"What he said is correct, sir. Mr. Burns seemed surprised that the buyer was his own decorator when we arrived at Britt's gallery. Not all the paintings he bought and commissioned are for Carrington, though," James explained. He was unsure of the comment about their personal relationship. Carl knew he was gay and didn't have an issue with him, but as Seth was a client, he worried that Carl would think it inappropriate.

"Yes, he explained that as well. Relax, son. I don't have a problem with all this. We don't produce the kind of artwork he explained was purchased so there's no argument about propriety."

As Carl spoke, Seth moved to stand beside James. He gently placed his hand on the small of James's back to show support and to help calm him a bit.

"James," Seth added when Carl paused. "I wanted Carl to know about *us* before someone else told him. I did not want there to be any issues or confusion. I hired Skye Designs, but our relationship is completely separate from your work here."

Before Seth or Carl could speak again, James heard Brian's nasty voice intrude. "How dare you bring one of your sick boy-toys up here, James? No one wants to see what kind of pervert you are or hang out with," Brian ranted. He didn't seem to realize who James was with, not that it lessened James's sheer mortification to have his supervisor talk to him like that in front of others. Especially Seth!

James stiffened, as did Seth and Carl. "Bri—Mr. West," James squeaked.

Seth turned to face the man who would dare to speak to James like that. "And just exactly who are you?" he snapped.

James noticed Carl had stepped back enough that Brian would not be able to see him right away.

"I am Brian West," he said, puffing up like the idiot bully he was. "This sick perv's soon-to-be ex-boss. We don't tolerate his or your kind around here. Now, get out before I call security. Both of you!"

"Ex-boss? What an appropriate title, Brian," Carl said as he rounded the corner again. James nearly burst from trying not to laugh at the look of sheer horror that flew across Brian's face when he realized who had overheard him attack James. "In fact, I would suggest that you head down to human resources right now. I'll have them cut you your final check and arrange for security to meet you in your *old* office.

"Now listen to me very carefully…. We do *not* tolerate hateful, narrow-minded, self-righteous, abusive people like you here. Oh, and the guy you just called his perverted boy-toy is Seth Burns. You know, the CEO of Carrington Enterprises. Good luck finding a new job."

chapter ten

ENTERING the restaurant, James blinked to allow his eyes to adjust to the dimmer lights. A slim, dimple-cheeked African American man with creamy light brown skin in a crisp white dress shirt and dark low-rise slacks met him at the hostess station.

"Hello, sir. Do you have a reservation?"

His eyes darted around the restaurant, then focused on the cute waiter in front of him. "I'm supposed to meet with Seth Burns. My name is James Bryant," James said, a slight tinge of nervousness leaking into his otherwise composed tone.

"Ah yes, Mr. Burns is awaiting you, I believe. Follow me, please."

James followed, as requested, admiring the way the server's slacks draped and slid against his form. There were candles on every table, each dressed with fine linen, spread out with ample space for James to maneuver and for each table to feel private. Light jazz music wafted softly around him as they approached a secluded alcove.

As they turned the corner, James got his first view of his date for the evening. He had seen Seth many times, in various stages of dress and undress, but there was nothing like that first glimpse of him in one of his tailored suits. The dark gray with a soft lavender dress shirt did amazing things for his changeable hazel eyes.

"James," Seth cooed, and a wicked smile spread across his handsome face. The look alone left James trembling inside and mute for a moment.

"Seth," he barely managed to force out. With a slightly stronger voice he continued, "Sorry I'm late."

With a gentle wave of his hand, Seth pushed away the apology as unnecessary. "You worry too much, sweetheart," Seth murmured. He stood, lightly brushed his lips across James's, and pulled the chair out for him.

Seth focused on James as he sat across from him at their small candlelit table at Terra's. "Before we settle into dinner too much, Britt asked me to speak to you. Let's get the business out of the way so we can enjoy the rest of our evening, baby."

James caught himself twisting his cloth napkin as he wondered what Seth and Britt wanted. "Yes, sir. Is something wrong?"

"No, James. Britt wants you to put in some extra work for her. She is planning an art show at the gallery and wants you to be one of her featured artists. However, she has sold all but one of your paintings, so she has a problem."

James nodded for Seth to continue.

"The theme is 'touch.' She feels that your art, with its 'visceral sensuality and erotic tones,' would be perfect, but that means you would have to focus on that for a bit. A gallery show means at least ten paintings, or so she stated."

"No, Seth," James contradicted. "It means at least twice that would need to be created so she could have the choice of which ones to place in the show. I may not have shown in recent times, but I do know how it works. You should always do more than what is requested because the gallery owner may not always like everything or, depending on the theme, may feel some work better fits than others." His art was one area that he knew what was what.

"So, that means you will do it?" Seth asked with an eager joy that surprised James.

"Depends on how long I have, Seth. It's not like business, you know. I have to not just do the *work* but I have to *create*. That takes time and inspiration, not just interest or desire. I work full time already on top of all the work Mr. Macey has commissioned."

They continued to discuss the show until the waiter returned with two glasses and the wine Seth ordered. Before the waiter could do more than set down the glasses and uncork the wine, Seth interrupted.

"I will pour for us. Thank you." His voice was soft but firm.

The waiter smiled, handed the linen-wrapped wine bottle to Seth, and quietly stepped away.

Seth poured a small amount into his glass. Cupping the crystal glass, he brought it to his lips and sipped. With a slow smile, he nodded to himself, then poured James a glass and topped off his.

James felt giddy as he watched Seth take such pride in caring for him. He knew what Seth said before about the ordering and such, but watching him gave James a strange sense of peace. He was certain he would never tire of Seth's attentions.

After a few silent moments, James looked up, meeting Seth's eyes. "Don't we need to order?" he asked. He wasn't ready to continue their talk, but his stomach was grumbling a little.

"I ordered before you arrived, James. They will bring out our appetizer and bread shortly." Seth smiled. His lips quirked up in a sensual yet slightly unnerving manner. "Now, tell me what you're thinking. Please."

James paused as he mulled over everything Seth had said. *Do a special set of paintings for a gallery show with Britt?* Turning a few ideas over, he frowned as he thought about the amount of work, of time, he would have to commit to make such a large project feasible.

"I don't know, Seth. I agree that the show would be a great opportunity, but I can't just quit my job at Skye Designs, nor is Carl going to allow me to go to part time. I've worked so hard to get what little I have there, and with Brian now gone, I might be able to get more stability and work. Maybe even move up some."

Even as he spoke, James knew he was only being partly honest with Seth and himself. He had never wanted to work in the business world like he did. He had always dreamt of having a little studio and living his life as an artist, where he only truly had to bend to the demands of an agent and the deadlines from various galleries that would sell his work. But until recently he had shut those desires down. Well, Victor had beaten his dreams out of him years ago, but now he wondered if he could break free and fully return to his art.

Seth stared back at him, piercing his thoughts and sending a shiver of desire curling through James's gut as those hazel eyes heated to encompass his very soul. Seth leaned forward enough to run his fingers up James's cheek and tenderly cup his face.

"Just think on the show and about speaking to Carl. You do not have to make a decision right now, but you need to live your life for you, not be boxed in by the fears and jealousy of those from your past," Seth said gently.

James tried to keep his fears hidden from Seth as much as possible, but now Seth suggested not only participating in the show but to possibly cut his hours at Skye Designs so he could focus more on his *real* art. On top of that, his heart ached, and his gut churned at the thought of actually having his dreams come true.

AFTER another dinner with Seth, this time with Seth cooking, James found himself too worked up to sleep. Giving up on that idea, he worked straight through the night. Inspiration hit and kept him sketching and painting until sometime earlier that morning, when he fell asleep in his work chair in the studio.

What woke him confused him. He lay still in the chair he used to paint, wondering why he was awake, though glad as sleeping there was never comfortable or smart. Just then he heard a sound by the doors on the other side of the room. The *tap, tap, tap* was followed by Chase's grumble. "Come on, Jamie. Wake up!"

James chuckled to himself as he stretched; trying to get rid of the horrid crick in his neck, then worked his way to standing.

"You have a key, Chase," James called out.

"Yeah, yeah, yeah. Now get over here, my hands are full."

As James finally maneuvered to the doors, he caught sight of Chase. There were shopping bags hanging off both wrists, a carrier with two coffee cups in one hand, and a small box held to his hip with the other.

He opened the door and moved out of Chase's way, pressing his lips together tightly as he fought to not laugh at both the picture Chase made in his doorway and at the disgruntled pout on his face.

"Finally! If I'd had my Bluetooth in I would have called your lazy ass to let me in instead of me traipsing around the house like some kind of demented burglar," Chase grumbled.

James watched as Chase stomped through his studio, and moments later heard the sound of things being set down, some not so gently. He made it to the kitchen doorway just in time to duck. Coming straight for his head had been an oven mitt, though he didn't make out what it was until he had ducked, and it landed behind him.

"Um, Chase? You want to tell me why you're acting like some sort of jilted harpy? What gives?"

"'What gives?' he asks," Chase muttered to himself. "You're really going to ask me that at ten in the morning? A Saturday morning, no less. If I didn't love you so much I'd strangle you right now," Chase replied. He walked over to James and thrust a Starbucks cup at him. "Here."

"Um, thanks, Chase." James's nose told him he held a mocha; with luck it would be white chocolate. He tasted: it was. *Mmm….*

"Now what is all this and why are you so pissed?"

"I get a call this morning from Carl. Did I mention it's Saturday morning?" Chase practically whined. "He says that since I act as your personal assistant at work so much, he wants me to do that more than my normal job. I don't mind that part, actually. But, then he starts in that he and your other boss, Mrs. Holcomb, need me to pick some things up for you and drop them off. Oh, and the lady boss will be by this afternoon."

"Wait. Britt and Carl are working together on something and sent you over here? What's in the bags, Chase?" James asked. He quickly moved over to the counter to start peeking through all the bags and the one box, in hopes of this conversation making sense sometime soon.

Chase simply waved at the pile with a *you figure it out* glower. What he found was almost as confusing as his wakeup had been. Paperwork—contracts he figured out quickly. New paints and a new set of expensive sable brushes in various sizes and styles. He even found new sketchpads and pencils.

While he investigated things, Chase continued, "The only reason I agreed to get up, much less come over this early, is Carl said you were going to be part of a gallery show. Is that true?" he practically squealed, finally looking something other than pissed off.

"Um, Seth asked me to on Britt's behalf, but I haven't given a definite yes to either of them. Wait, why is Carl in on this?" James wondered aloud. He paused in digging through the new materials to pull out his cell. After hitting number two—Seth's speed dial number—James waited, drumming his fingers on the countertop.

"Good morning, pet" came Seth's deep, melodious voice.

"Morning, Seth. Don't suppose you know why Chase is standing in my kitchen this morning?" James snapped. It came out a bit harsher than he had intended, but he suddenly felt like he was being forced into a commitment prematurely. They had discussed the show at dinner the night before last.

He promised to think about it. He even stayed up all night, thanks to inspiration, to work on a piece he thought would be perfect. But he had not agreed to anything yet and did not appreciate the not-so-subtle push.

"I would assume your best friend is there to visit you. Hang out, maybe. But, baby, why are you asking me instead of him?" Seth replied. He sounded almost as confused as James felt.

"Seth, he says that Carl and Britt sent him because of the show they think I agreed to do. Oh, and do you know why Carl is even party to this?" James knew he was probably being an idiot, but he couldn't rein in his irritation.

"I told Britt that you said 'maybe.' I never told her yes and I have no clue about your boss. I'll call Britt and ask her what's going on. I will stop by in a bit. Okay?" Seth's take charge attitude and soothing voice, as always, calmed James, leaving him wanting Seth yet comforted at the same time.

"Yes, sir. And Seth? Sorry for yelling at you."

"It's okay, baby. I will be over in a little bit. For now, why don't you go have some fun with Chase?"

LATER that day James, Chase, and Seth sat on the back patio, discussing the show and Britt and Carl's behavior.

Chase said with a laugh, "I can't believe that Mrs. Holcomb got Carl's wife to make him help her corner you into doing the show." He was slightly tipsy, thanks to the Long Island Iced Teas he consumed, and continued to consume.

Seth countered with a chuckle, "Chase, never underestimate a smart woman with conviction and more than three-inch high heels. I learned that the hard way when I was a teenager."

"Ha-ha. Seth, dear, I never underestimate *any*one wearing heels of three or more inches," Chase countered, giggling by the end.

"Hmm, true. But, in Britt's case, she's deadly whether in heels or her fuzzy bunny slippers. Trust me."

"Seth, I'm still worried about all this. This is a huge project, not as much time as I would like beforehand, and no matter that you technically asked, they're trying to not give me a choice in the matter."

"Jamie," Chase interrupted, "you want to do art. You want to do the show. We all know that's your real love, so why are you being so prissy, hun? I mean, you're not going to turn down the show just to piss them off for pressuring you, are you?"

"Well, um, no. I mean, yes I want to do the show. That was never the question, Chase. I don't know that I have the talent to compete with her other artists or the time to do the work right. You know how time-consuming my art can be and she's asking for at least ten new paintings. That's ten beyond the ones that Seth's buyer, Zach, has already commissioned. Plus, I have work still with Carl at Skye Designs." He knew he was rambling again, but James didn't have the restraint or the faith in his abilities that the other two seemed to have.

"James, do you think I would suggest you do something that was honestly beyond your abilities? That I would ask you to do something that I didn't firmly believe you could do?" Seth asked, his voice soft but earnest.

"No, sir. You wouldn't do that to me. I know that, but I don't see how I can dream and be responsible at the same time."

"I only want to encourage your dreams and support you however I may. You have to decide if you want this or not. I won't push, or I will try not to at least, but I will encourage you to take back your life completely and be who you are meant to be."

James nodded. He tilted his head to the side as he looked Seth over. "I still don't understand why she always goes to you instead of speaking directly to me about all these things. She's treating you like you're my agent or something."

"I believe that is how she sees it as well. I will ask her to go to you instead if you prefer, baby," Seth explained.

"No, I don't mind. I was a little confused but"—James's voice dropped to a whisper—"I kinda like you being so involved."

chapter eleven

STEAMING water poured over his tight shoulders as James groaned softly, soaking in the heat to soothe the tense muscles in his back and shoulders. The driving pressure from the high-powered showerhead was a pleasure, an indulgent one, that he was thankful Chase talked him into.

James relaxed as his eyes fluttered closed, and he released a deep sigh. He let the water wash away the tension and stress from his physical therapy session. He loved his shower, preferred it to the one at the therapy center he had just come from.

Shifting his attention from the luscious heat, he opened his eyes and swiped the water from his face when he heard the bathroom door open. Straightening, James leaned forward so he could open the edge of his shower and peer into the main part of the room. His attention was immediately caught by the sight of his handsome lover leaning casually against the doorway a few feet away.

Seth was breathtaking as he braced one shoulder against the doorjamb, his arms folded across his broad, powerful chest and his right leg bent so his ankles crossed. He was the picture of laid-back ease in nothing but slightly distressed jeans and a well-worn, soft T-shirt.

James quickly ducked back in to shut off the water. He opened the shower door, dried off, and wrapped one of his oversized bath sheets around his waist, before he carefully maneuvered himself over to where Seth stood.

"You're early, Seth," James murmured, not quite meeting Seth's devouring gaze.

"I think I am right on time, personally," Seth replied as he threaded his fingers through James's damp hair.

"How did you get in?"

"You gave me a key last night, or did you forget already?" Seth asked as his eyes continued to roam James's glistening body.

As he brushed his lips against Seth's, James sighed, "Right." Seth flicked his tongue out to wet James's parted lips before he could pull back. He moved his hands over James's body as he pulled James closer.

James took the moment in and then slowly slipped his hands up Seth's chest before he wrapped his arms loosely around Seth's neck. He met Seth's heated eyes for a second, then leaned in again and kissed him, lingering yet with only the barest of pressure.

Seth slid his arms around James. He could feel Seth's cock filling even more as their bodies moved together.

James whimpered when Seth shifted to grind their hips together and arched his back to help increase the pressure. Seth's hands slid down to cup James's ass through the towel that sat precariously low on his hips. As he deepened the kiss, Seth kneaded the fleshy globes that he gently gripped in his large hands.

James carded his fingers through Seth's soft hair and drank in the ever-deepening kiss, waiting for Seth to decide how to progress. It wasn't that he didn't care or have ideas of what he would like to do with Seth, but he had found he truly enjoyed giving more and more control to Seth—not that he was about to tell Seth. When Seth tilted his head back, breaking the kiss for a moment, James moved his lips down across Seth's jaw to lick and tease along his throat. Emboldened by Seth's responses, James nipped at his pulse and tugged on his hair playfully.

"Oh, has my pet decided he wants to play a little rougher?" Seth's voice rumbled deep in his chest as he bent to drag his lips across James's throat, and nip a bit harder than James had nipped him—enough to stimulate with a small sting, not to actually hurt. James could only manage another whimper.

Seth groaned; it sounded almost painful and drew out more little noises from James. He moved to capture James's lips and deepen the kiss as he rocked against James more.

"Hold on tight, baby," Seth ordered as he lifted James and demanded he wrap his legs around his hips. He turned from the doorway and worked his way to the edge of the bed. Once he stood James up, he kissed him again, enticing more whimpers and mewls from James. He stopped long enough to kiss and suck down James's neck and across his shoulders, marking his pale skin. James tilted his head to allow more room for Seth's sensual assault, moaning wantonly as he slid his fingers down Seth's chest to pull up the T-shirt.

James wasn't having much luck with the shirt, not with how hard his fingers were trembling. His need for Seth eclipsed every other thought in his mind. He was so aroused his soul ached and his mind swam with thoughts and memories of what he wanted Seth to do and what he had done before.

Seth finally took mercy on James and quickly pulled his shirt off and wrapped his arms back around James, pressing their naked skin together. He kissed across his jaw, then moved to trace the shell of James's ear before lightly flicking his tongue against the point behind it that made James tremble every time.

"Seth," James nearly whined as he pushed at Seth's jeans, desperate to feel all of Seth against him. With only a little fumbling, Seth unbuttoned his jeans and pushed them down his hips, then pulled off the towel that had somehow managed to still cling to James's slim hips.

James looked down at Seth's body and noted with pleasure that Seth had nothing on underneath his jeans and was fully hard. He knew what he felt, but seeing Seth's enticing body made his mouth water. His knees bent of their own accord as his hand captured Seth's erection.

Seth's hands shot out to grasp James's arms, halting his descent. "No, baby. Middle of the bed, on your back. I want to admire your body right now."

James quickly moved into the center of his large bed, stretched out to allow Seth complete access to his body. He looked up from under his lashes to gaze at his pleasantly demanding lover. He was a little nervous about how much he wanted to please Seth and about how attached he was becoming to Seth. But right then, he couldn't care about anything except how much he wanted Seth inside him.

Seth smiled and watched James obey. James licked his lips as he watched Seth smile and spread his now bent legs, giving Seth a wonderful view of his hungry, throbbing entrance.

Seth slowly crawled up the bed until he could stretch out and completely cover James.

James groaned in frustration as Seth pressed his body into his and devoured his mouth. James shivered and mewled against Seth as his desperation reached a breaking point. He pushed up into Seth and wrapped his hands around Seth's hips, forcing their cocks together. "Please, Seth. Fill me, use me. Fuck me, damn it! Please," he begged.

Seth gripped his hair and pulled hard, arching his head back to look into his eyes. "You are *not* some*thing* to use, baby. You *are* some*one* to cherish."

James was so startled by both the rough handling and what Seth had said that he merely nodded and rocked up into Seth, using his body to beg for more.

James swallowed hard as Seth began making his way down his body instead of commenting more, kissing and nipping at sensitive parts. James stiffened when Seth flicked his tongue out to catch the pearl drop at the tip of his slit. His hips snapped toward the unbelievable wet heat of Seth's mouth as he suddenly engulfed James's throbbing cock. James nearly came with the first hard suck he was so desperate for his lover.

A blast of pure joy threatened to drown James when he felt the first touch of Seth's nimble fingers at his entrance. He rocked helplessly between Seth's hot mouth and his ever more penetrating digits, crying out continually as Seth pummeled his sweet spot and seemed determined to devour him whole.

James fought against his body's desire to release, determined to have Seth fill him before he came. He rocked helplessly but managed to pull enough at Seth to get him to release his hold. James couldn't help how his body trembled and writhed shamelessly as he gasped and begged. "Please, Seth. Fuck... in me, please. I can't...."

"You sure, baby?" Seth asked. His voice was low, barely more than a growl.

"Please, yes!" he keened as Seth dug in his fingers and flipped James over, pulled him up on his knees. As James braced himself, arms under his upper body, Seth placed a hand on his lower back, effectively holding him in place.

Seth quickly rolled on a condom and slicked himself before he aligned his cock. Pushing carefully, Seth rocked against James's fluttering hole, slowly driving his way inside. Seth curled his body over James, and bent to kiss his nape as he reached around and wrapped his fingers around James's bobbing cock. He began to snap his hips to the same rhythm as he stroked James, providing a double assault of friction and pleasure that quickly sent James over the edge.

The pleasure was so sharp as James's tight body rippled and spasmed around Seth that it ripped his own orgasm from him before he wanted to give in. With a strangled cry, he drove into James, pumping his hips through the aftershocks of James's release as well as his own.

James exhaled and shook, unable to move. The mind-devouring orgasm left James whimpering and panting against his arms.

As the world again settled around Seth, he trailed wet, open-mouthed kisses across James's shoulders and back before he shifted to pull out. James clenched his fingers and squeezed convulsively around Seth, drawing a whimpered gasp from him. It was both pain and pleasure as Seth finally slid out, leaving them both aching yet blissful.

Seth shifted to tend to the condom before he slowly rolled them over to their sides. Sweaty and replete, he spooned his body around James, lightly stroking his arm, chest, shoulder, and hair as James continued to tremble sporadically.

After an indeterminate time, James shifted back to press himself tighter against Seth. "That...."

"I didn't hurt you, did I?" Seth asked.

"Hurt?" James asked, confused. "No, you were perfect, Seth." He smiled, though Seth couldn't see it, and lifted Seth's hand, pressing a soft kiss to his knuckles before he curled his arm around Seth's hand and tucked it under his cheek. With a sigh he let his body settle against Seth's broad chest, content to stay like that as long as Seth would allow.

"Love you, baby," Seth mumbled as sleep embraced them.

JAMES barely managed to find his way to wakefulness when Seth's phone trilled demandingly in the other room. He jerked slightly when Seth suddenly hopped out of bed and hurried out of the bedroom.

James grinned but managed to stifle the giggle that nearly burst forth at the comical sight of his lover, tangled in the sheet, trying to run while hopping. He contemplated staying where he was, but with how animated Seth had been, he figured snuggling and sleeping were probably out now. He'd really been looking forward to snuggling back into Seth and another round of sex. With a sigh, he sat up and looked around for his crutches before he remembered that Seth had carried him to bed.

Moments later Seth paced back in the room and ducked into the ensuite, retrieving James's forearm crutches and talking on the phone. James kept quiet as he watched and listened to his obviously upset lover.

"When?" Seth snapped. The tension radiating off him was like a physical force in the room. "Yeah, I'll be there as soon as I can." He listened for a few more moments. "Do *not* let anyone in to see her until I get there. *No one!*" he snapped at whoever was on the other end of the line. "Yes, thank you. Be there in ten minutes," Seth finished, and then clicked his cell off.

"Oh God. That was the hospital. My little sister was just brought in and they aren't sure she'll make it. I...." Seth trailed off. He continued his whirlwind around the room, grabbing his clothes and quickly dressing.

"Seth," James said softly. "Do you want me to come with you? I could drive." He hoped Seth would say yes—he wanted to be there for Seth—but he feared that the answer would be no. It was a family situation after all.

"Huh?" Seth mumbled as he pulled his shirt over his head. "Oh, come with...? Uh, if you want but it's just going to be a lot of pacing and waiting for someone you don't know."

"Tell me where we're going. I don't want to delay you with my lack of speed, but you shouldn't be alone, Seth," James explained as he stood and headed for his dresser. Seth was already dressed and headed toward the door before James retrieved clean clothes to put on.

James dressed quickly and they headed out immediately. He worried about Seth and his sister—a sister he had never met.

Valet parking was a godsend in James's opinion, especially right then.

"Tell me where you're going and I'll meet you there."

Seth paused with the door already open. "Emergency surgery. Just ask at the counter when you get there. Cell phones have to be off up there. I gotta.... Thanks," he trailed off and took off.

He wanted to be with Seth, now. Even more so at the thought the news might be bad. No one should get bad news alone, though he figured Seth's friends might already be there. He also felt that as Seth's lover, he should be there for him, no matter what the news was. He really hoped it would be good.

As he headed for emergency surgery, he thought back to when it had been him rushed to surgery and Chase had been the one pacing the waiting room. Chase had always sworn that having his friends around while they awaited news made the hours bearable. He hoped the same would be true for Seth.

As he stepped off the elevator, James noticed Mel rushing down the hall with an empty wheelchair. "James! Your chariot awaits, hurry."

Mel continued to hurry and spun the chair around next to James, practically shoving him into it, before he grabbed James's crutches and went barreling down the hall again.

"Wait! What are you doing, Mel?" James demanded as he was manhandled and driven away.

"Seth said you were on your way. He's stopped talking already. He just paces and glowers at the doors. Well, and growls when anyone gets near him. I'm hoping that having you here will help steady him."

"I got in here as fast as I could, Mel. I wanted to come in with him but," James said as he gestured to his legs and crutches.

"Understood, James. He needs you. We need you. If Quinn, if she doesn't make it, he's going to lose it. He calls her his sister. They're that close. I can't even imagine how bad this will be for him."

Before James or Mel could talk more, they rounded the corner to the waiting area. Seth was pacing, just as Mel had said, but the dark look on his face caused James to draw in a pained breath. The look wasn't scared or worried as much as it was murderous. He knew that look. It was the same one Chase had when he learned the extent of how the "accident" happened and about the lies Vic had told to escape any blame.

James maneuvered over to Seth, cautious so he didn't block his pacing. "Seth?" he said softly.

Seth paused and looked up. "James? You came?" he queried. His head tilted as his face blanked in confusion.

"Of course, Seth. I told you I would be right behind you." James moved to Seth's side and wrapped his arms around him for a moment, hoping to provide some support if nothing else. "Do we know anything yet?"

"Nothing. All I know is that Danni was with friends when this happened so at least she wasn't hurt too. Oh God, Mel. We have to go get Danni. If—if…," Seth choked, unable to finish his thought.

"Seth, I called Britt. She and her assistant Bryce are on their way to pick up Danni. You'll have a full waiting room of her friends and yours shortly, but until then, you have James and me. Danni's a big girl and she knows Britt. Don't worry," Mel soothed.

James looked over to Mel as he guided Seth to the chairs and mouthed, *"Who's Danni?"*

"Danni is Quinn and Seth's daughter," Mel whispered back.

chapter twelve

QUINN and Seth's daughter? Seth has a daughter?

Even as James continued to hold Seth and provide comfort as best he could, he tensed and wondered what else he didn't know that might be important. He knew Seth had a history, but a kid? With someone he referred to as his sister?

Before James worked up the courage to ask Seth anything, Britt entered the waiting area. A moment later an adorable little girl of maybe six bounced into the room, closely followed by a tall, powerfully built man—Bryce, he presumed.

The little girl bounded right over to where Seth now sat, her red pigtails swinging with every movement. "Unca Seth, why you look so sad?" Danni asked as she put her little hands on his cheeks, forcing him to look up at her. Her voice was high and sweet, and made James immediately think of bubble gum and ponies.

"Hi, princess," Seth replied, his voice a little wooden. He scooped her up and held her close. "Do you know why we are here?"

"Auntie Britt said mommy was sick, and we had to come here to see her. When can I see mommy?"

"I don't know, Danni. We are waiting for the doctor to come tell us how your mommy is. Do you need anything to eat or drink?" Seth asked the little girl. "Do you know if she's eaten yet, Britt?" he asked, turning to face Britt.

"Yes, and I have some snacks and even a couple of juice boxes. Relax, Seth. I have raised a couple of kids of my own, ya know." Her voice was chipper, though James could see the worry and pain in her eyes.

Seth nodded to her as he shifted Danni sideways. James paused, not sure if he should sit next to Seth or not. Did the little girl, his daughter, know her daddy was gay? Would it be appropriate? More importantly, did Seth even want him to be there? With the way Seth had greeted him, he wasn't sure.

"James, come down here," Seth said, his voice barely above a whisper.

As James settled in the chair next to Seth, Danni looked him over carefully. "Why you have those funny things on your arms? Did you get hurt too, mister?"

Despite his irritation at not having known she existed and fear for Seth and Quinn, James was enchanted by the cute little pixie primly perched on his lover's lap. "No, sweetie. My legs don't work quite right so I use these to help me walk. Don't worry." He set the forearm crutches aside and extended his hand to her. "I'm James. A friend of...." James paused a moment to think of what to call Seth.

"He's my boyfriend, princess," Seth interjected.

"Oh, he's cute, Unca Seth," she chirped, then suddenly leaned forward, landing in James's lap, her arms wrapped around his neck. "Hi," Danni sang.

Uff. "Um, hi." James nearly chuckled.

"Well, looks like you pass the kid test," Britt commented with a soft smile. "Though you, little miss, shouldn't launch yourself at people you don't know."

"But Unca Seth said he was his boyfriend," she insisted with a pout. "My Unca wouldn't date a bad man," Danni said with all the conviction a six-year-old could muster. Even though James wanted to be upset, he just couldn't. She was so adorable!

"It's okay, Britt. Danni didn't hurt me." As James shifted her so it wouldn't be a lie, a man in scrubs entered the waiting area. The green scrubs were rumpled, and the man's expression was serious as he looked around.

"Seth Burns?" the man's clear voice called out. Seth was up and over to him faster than James could hardly process.

"I'm Seth."

"Dr. Greene," the man replied and extended his hand. Seth shook it on autopilot. The two men moved to just outside the doors. James could only hear snippets of the conversation, but the "I'm sorry, sir" and Seth's tears and shoulders shaking made it obvious that the news wasn't good. James did what he could to keep the little one in his lap busy and distracted. Those in the know needed to be the ones to tell her what was happening, not her overhearing things.

JAMES found Seth in his arms shortly thereafter, the others having cleared out, Danni included. Mel was the only other person still there.

"Seth," Mel said softly. "I know you don't want to talk about this yet, but we need to start proceedings as soon as possible. To protect Danni."

Seth nodded but didn't let go of James. "I know, but you have all her papers; the paternity affidavit, her will, and…. Can't you just file? You're the lawyer."

"Yes, Seth. I am the lawyer that drew up everything, but I need to know if you are really able and willing to take Danni and raise her. When you agreed to this no one thought you would actually have to raise her. You were simply the surrogate and Uncle, now you have to be both mom and dad for your little princess."

Seth's head snapped up, a cold expression in his eyes. "I am well aware of what I agreed to and what I expected. Danni is my daughter, period. I will, I will make it work. Her things can be moved over to my—"

"You don't have a guest bedroom in your condo, Seth," Mel countered.

"I do," James whispered. "You could keep her at my place until you can figure out what to do. I-if, if you want."

Mel and Seth both turned to look at James. "At your house?" Seth asked, his tone flat, yet his eyes were shadowed in confusion.

"I've been to your condo, Seth. Mel's right. It's not set up to handle a lively little girl. You don't have a room for her. There's no yard for her to play…." He trailed off. He swallowed hard, looking down at his shoes, and then added, "I'm sorry. I'll be quiet now." He couldn't believe he'd spoken up like that. Like Seth would want to move him and his new daughter into his stone cottage-type home, even temporarily. Ha!

"Those are good points, Seth. At least until you can provide a better situation, if you want. Quinn's parents are likely to fight this, you know that. You need to show how well you understand and can cater to her needs. You already provide things like her private school, but children need love and a home much more than fancy schools or expensive clothes."

"But that cottage is James's home," Seth stated firmly. "I will not just take it over to simply attempt to look good to people who hate me. There is nothing in my life that they can use to show I'm not capable of caring for Danni."

Mel arched his back and several vertebrae popped. He relaxed in relief before opening his eyes to take in Seth's scowl. "Seth, I never said you should take over James's house, nor did I say your life was in any way lacking. What I said was that your condo is not suited to your new situation, and as your lover here pointed out, his place would be better for a little one."

"If you don't want her exposed to *us* or don't want to risk her getting too attached to me, I can ask Chase to let me stay with him until you can find a new place. Your place is great for a bachelor or maybe even a childless couple, but—" James paused to take a deep breath. "—but I think she would be happier in a house with a yard and her own room," he finally added in a whisper.

"James, *we* don't even live together, and now you are offering to move both me and my child in? A child you did not even know about until today? Why? Why would you do that?" Seth watched him intently, though James was uncertain what he found.

"He's right, James. This would be a huge change for you," Mel added. Only James noticed the hopeful gleam in his eyes as he looked between the two men.

James nodded slowly. "I would really like to ask a million questions about Danni and her mom, and why you never told me you had a kid, but right now taking care of your daughter is more important than placating my worries or questions. And, well, you're always there for me...." Slowly meeting Seth's inquisitive eyes, James swallowed and added softly, "Let me be your shoulder and partner, please."

"YOU did what?" Chase squeaked.

Jaw tight, James set his glass down with such force the juice he had just poured splashed out, making his hand and shirt wet and sticky. "Invited Seth and Danni to move in, at least for now," James explained for the third time. "What else was I supposed to do, Chase?"

"I don't know.... Demand to know why he's not bothered to tell you he had a kid," Chase snapped. "I mean, you two have been together long enough that something that important should have been discussed. And what about this ex or sorta-sister or whatever the hell the mom was?"

"I don't know yet, but Mel said something about Seth being her surrogate. I couldn't ask right then. He obviously cared for this woman, and she'd just died. Right then was not the time to act the jealous boyfriend."

"Maybe, but now you've got someone else's kid living in your home," Chase murmured, finally winding down a bit. "I just worry about you, Jamie. A kid that age is going to be hell on your mobility, and what about your art? She's too young to be allowed near most of your work."

"I'll figure it out. I can't not be there for Seth. Chase. I think I love him. Kid aside, he shouldn't be alone, and I—I want to be the one to help him. Do you really think I did the wrong thing?"

"No," Chase answered with a sigh. "I would probably do the same if I found someone as great as you have. I just worry and well, ignore me. How old is the kid and what does she like?"

"She's six and seems very girly. You know, pigtails and ponies, and she wore a lot of pink. Why?"

"Because, your house isn't set up for her yet so I'll go shopping and be back later," he explained. As he headed out, leaving James confused and nervous, he could be heard mumbling. "Six. Girl. Right, pink and dolls and like frilly stuff, probably."

James set to cleaning up the mess, and then headed toward his bedroom to change when the doorbell rang. He'd gotten as far as taking off his shirt but not putting a new one on. With the ringing being so insistent, he hurried on his crutches back out front in just his jeans.

"Chase, did you forget your keys again?" James asked as he opened the door.

Instead of Chase he found Seth and the pixie-sized Danni standing there. She clutched Seth's hand with one of hers while her other hand had a death grip on a stuffed, pastel tie-dyed bunny in a tiny white and green Irish dancing dress with miniature black Mary Janes. The bright-eyed happy imp of a girl was gone, and in her place was a puffy eyed, sad little waif.

"Hi, James. You still want us to stay with you?" Seth's voice was soft, tired and sad but still cautious as he looked from James to Danni and back.

"Of course I do." James tore his eyes away from Seth and locked onto Danni's. "Let me finish getting dressed and then we can get Danni settled."

Danni looked up at him with big doe eyes. "Thank you, Mr. James. Can Ms. Rainbow stay too?" Her light earnest voice and trembling bottom lip broke James's heart.

"Ms. Rainbow can stay as long as she wants. Does she need her own bed or is she going to stay with you, sweetie?"

"With me." A small smile spread across her little heart-shaped face.

James returned her smile. "Good. Then why don't you and your daddy, um uncle—" he corrected quickly, "—go pick out which room will be yours, and I'll come find you two in a minute?" James looked back up to Seth, cautious. "That work for you, sir?"

"Of course, baby. And James, thank you."

James left them to explore the two guest rooms. He finished dressing, wondering how long Seth would want to stay. He secretly hoped they never left even as he questioned if he would really be able to handle the new living arrangements.

As SETH came back from settling Danni in the bedroom beside James's studio—across the house from his bedroom—Chase stood. "I should let you two have some time together now that the little one is asleep. I'm glad she liked the stuff I brought over, but you both look beat." Chase leaned over to hug James, then offered his hand to Seth. "I'll stop by in the morning, okay?"

They both agreed. Seth walked Chase out but came right back.

"You ready for bed, Seth?"

"Not sure I will actually be able to sleep but yes," Seth answered. He bent to kiss James's lips lightly, then moved back to allow him space to get off the couch.

Once in his, now their, bedroom, they each took turns cleaning up and dressing for bed. James in sleep pants and a worn T-shirt, Seth in sleep pants only.

For the first time, James pulled Seth to him, wrapped his arms around him, and tucked the covers around them both.

"James," Seth said after an indeterminate time.

"Hmm?"

"What are we doing?"

Carding his fingers repeatedly through Seth's hair, James thought for a moment before he replied. "We're going to sleep. You need to rest, Seth. I left the door open in case Danni wakes up and needs you, so don't worry. I told her she can come in if she wants to. Now, close your eyes, please."

"Thanks but that wasn't what I meant, baby. Why are we here? You should be angry with me, not taking in a kid you only met today." It was too dark for James to see much, but the tension in Seth's body combined with his voice spoke volumes.

"I'm sure you will explain Danni and her mom to me when you are ready. For now, loving you means accepting and caring for your daughter as well. I can be patient."

After another pregnant pause, Seth propped up on an elbow, staring down at James intently. "You... you love me?"

With a shrug and nervous cough, James reached up to touch Seth's lips gently. Not quite how he had envisioned admitting that to Seth, but, "Um, yes. I do. I... wish I'd known about Danni, but I—I love you, Seth." He held his breath as he awaited Seth's response.

"I—I think...," he stuttered, then paused. James immediately pulled him down again, wrapping around him as he silently shook. He hadn't expected a great declaration of love but knew deep down that no matter what Seth felt, or didn't feel, now was not the time. James wasn't sure what to do, think, or hardly even how to breathe, but he was certain that Seth being there with him was right. Danni too.

"Baby? You okay?"

James nodded against Seth's temple. "Rest, love," he crooned. He hoped Seth would listen for once and rest. He knew he would not sleep any time soon, but holding Seth was something he could do for him.

JAMES lay awake, listening to the steady breathing of his lover, his love, late into the night. So many thoughts tumbled around in his head, and his heart ached, but he was certain of his choices and direction as far as moving Seth and Danni in. He was unsure how her presence would change their relationship, change how Seth behaved toward him, but he didn't see any other choice. He silently wished he could call his mom and ask her advice, but he knew how well that would go over. Hell, she would probably help Quinn's parents try to take the little pixie away from them if he talked to her.

He was pulled from his depressing thoughts by a small voice and a sniffle. "Unca—Daddy, I don't wanna be alone. Ms. Rainbow's scared," Danni whispered.

James sat up slowly, so as to not scare her. "Your daddy's right here. Come here and I'll tuck you in beside him, okay?"

She sniffled and nodded, tiptoeing over to the edge of the big bed. James bent and scooped her up, shifting to place her between him and Seth. "Here, you can have my pillow, sweetie. I was going to get up anyway. Do you need anything before I head out?"

She shook her head and curled up against Seth, clutching her bunny as she settled.

James bent again and kissed her forehead. "Try to sleep, Danni."

Just before he entered his studio, he paused at the door to Danni's room. Chase had brought dolls, toys, and some play clothes, but what caught him right then was the baby monitor his friend had also bought. Chase had insisted that until she recovered some from the loss and got used to living with them, the monitor would help them keep tabs on her at night, like if she was crying or anything. James moved into the room and picked up the monitor, thinking that maybe both Seth and Danni might need to be watched and cared for right then.

Moving as silently as he could manage, James put the monitor on his nightstand and took the receiver part with him. He needed to paint, to get his feelings out right then, but this way he could also feel secure that he was doing what was needed for Seth and Danni.

chapter thirteen

"HEY, Danni? What do you think we should make for dinner?" James asked. He had taken a few days off to stay home with her while she adjusted to living with him and Seth, and to the loss of her mother. Seth had a harder time taking time; being a CEO meant his company needed him actively there more, and since James's only active client was Carrington, it made sense. To him, at least.

Danni perched carefully on one of the tall stools in James's kitchen and watched everything he did. They had already covered why he used his forearm crutches and why he had a special stool with wheels, and that no, she was not allowed to play with it. "Hmm, I think he would like pizza," she finally answered, her little legs swinging back and forth as she beamed up at him.

"Pizza? Hmm… that sounds more like something a six-year-old pixie would like," he countered, though he knew Seth did, in fact, like pizza—he preferred the fancy ones from a specialty pizza shop across town.

"He likes pizza too, Mr. James," she countered. "But, he puts weird things on his," she explained in a near whisper, her little nose wrinkled in obvious displeasure. "Could we make two?"

James feared for whomever she set her sights on when she got older. They would have no defense against those big blue-gray eyes and her little dimples. She had him wrapped already, and he knew it.

"Alright, but only if you promise to set the table and wash your hands before we eat. Seth should be home soon." *Home*, he mused. He again wondered how long they would stay.

"I promise. I'm good at setting the table." She grinned up at him again.

With a *thank you* he sent her off to play while he worked. As requested, he made two, one a white seafood pizza and the other plain cheese—Danni had explained that anything but cheese on a pizza was "gross." He'd been hard pressed not to laugh, but didn't think she would appreciate his amusement. He was, however, happy that she had spent the last half hour or so not crying, quiet, or clinging to him for dear life.

He had just put the pizzas in the oven when he heard the front door open and close. "James?" Seth called out.

"Kitchen." He was cleaning up when Seth made it to where he was.

"Oh, what did you make? And how is Danni?" Seth asked between kisses. He slid both arms around James's waist but kept the kiss gentle and loose.

"Mmm, I'll have to make pizza more often if that's the reward I get," James teased. "Danni is in her room playing. Chase bought her more stuff to play with. A house and car for her dolls and such. I don't know. He insisted it was all things a girl her age would like and by the smile on her face when he showed her the goodies, I'm guessing he was right."

"He's going to spoil her, you know." It was a statement, though there was no heat to his words.

"Yeah, but as he pointed out, he's never had a niece to dote on before, and that I would be cruel not to let him enjoy it a little."

"She needs the cheering up, so okay. For now," Seth added. He pulled away finally and headed to the fridge, pulled out two waters, and offered James one.

"How long before we can get her properly moved in?" James asked tentatively once he'd taken a sip. He didn't want to push, but he also did not want Seth to only stay a few days.

"Her things will arrive tomorrow, baby," Seth explained. "Mel and Britt supervised the movers as they packed up today. The movers will be here first thing in the morning. And don't worry, they will move and set everything up for her, including removing the furniture that is in there now. All you have to do is direct and sign off once it's done."

He slid his stool so Seth was between his knees and wrapped his hands around his waist, settling his hands at the small of Seth's back, a reversal of their welcome home hug. With a slight tilt to his head, James took in how Seth stood and the dark circles under his eyes. As he carded his fingers through Seth's hair gently, he suggested, "Why don't you go sit down and rest while I finish dinner. Danni's going to set the table in a few, so all you need to do is show up and eat."

"You do not have to baby me, James."

"True, but you're tired and hurting. I have the salad made— blackberry spinach, by the way—the bread cooling, and the pizza in. There's nothing left to do, lo—Seth."

Seth's eyes narrowed as he pressed forward, tighter against James. "What were you going to say?"

James quickly looked away, embarrassed by his slip up. He had been surprised the previous night when Seth hadn't chastised him for using something other than his name or sir. Now he'd done it again. "Nothing," he murmured quickly.

"James," Seth snapped.

"Love," he whispered. "I was going to call you love. I'm sorry. I won't do it again." James fell silent once done speaking and pulled away, afraid.

Seth's face softened, his eyes shining with unshed tears that he tried to blink back. "You called me that last night, just before I fell asleep."

James swallowed hard. He'd hoped Seth had missed his little slip. With a slight nod, he said, "Yes, sir. I'll be more careful. I promise."

"Why are you shaking, baby? I love that you want to call me that." Seth closed his eyes for a moment. Finally he asked, "Are you expecting me to be angry with you?"

His eyes riveted on Seth, James watched as conflicting emotions flitted across his beloved face. He nodded.

"Why?"

"Pet names are not something… I got hit if I called Victor anything other than Victor or Vic. He said it wasn't my place to mess with his name. I—"

"James, baby," Seth interrupted. "I love that you want to call me that! I keep wondering why you only call me by my name or once in a while, sir. Which is hot by the way," he added with a smirk. "Your ex was an idiot. Period," Seth added as he pulled James into a tight hug. Sliding his hand around James's neck, he squeezed gently.

James continued to tremble, but now for an entirely different reason. *Seth likes when I called him* sir *and* love? He couldn't believe the endearment *love* was allowed—it surprised and pleased him.

He took a moment to steady himself before he spoke again.

"Then, there's nothing left for you to do, love. You should check on Danni and rest," James advised. He watched carefully for how Seth reacted.

"There, now that wasn't so difficult, was it?" Seth teased. "But—" Seth's words were cut off by the shrill ringing of the oven timer. They both laughed at the timing.

Seth pulled the pizzas out of the oven while James got the plates and retrieved the necessary silverware.

"Princess," Seth called. "Hands washed, please. And I believe you told James you would set the table."

Danni bounded in the room, holding up still wet but thankfully clean hands. "Good girl," James praised. He handed her a paper towel to dry her hands, then pointed out the items she needed for the table.

He was pleased to see that he only needed to correct her fork placement.

However, James was sorry to note that Seth and Danni were quiet during dinner, and both only picked at their food. He wondered if the lack of appetite was solely due to their shared loss or if he should have ordered out.

Shortly after dinner, Seth put Danni to bed. Instead of heading into the great room or toward their bed, Seth wandered outside. James could see him standing on the patio from his vantage point in the kitchen as he put things away. He decided to take a chance and poured a couple of fingers of the expensive Dalmore Whisky Seth had bought and took it out to him—having long ago perfected how to carry drinks with his crutches.

"Seth," he inquired softly. He didn't want to interrupt him if he needed alone time, but he didn't really want Seth to be alone either. He could see the pain and loss in Seth's eyes, though he had no idea how to help.

Seth turned slowly, not meeting his eyes but looking in his general direction. James noticed the tears that streaked his face. Instead of speaking, James simply held out the whisky in a silent offering.

It took a few moments, but Seth finally moved over to where James stood and accepted the drink. After he took a sip, he met James's worried eyes. "Sit with me?" he asked so softly James almost missed the words.

"I'd like that." A gentle breeze caressed his face.

Once they had settled on the swing together, James wrapped his arms around Seth. He stayed silent as he waited for Seth to decide what he wanted to do.

After an eternity of nothing but the crickets chirping, Seth spoke. "I can't believe she's gone, James. I've known Quinn my whole life. Even when I left home at fifteen for college we kept in touch. I can't remember a time she did not exist in my life. And now...." He trailed off, an audible sob the only sound he made for a time.

"You don't have to talk about her yet if you're not ready. I can just hold you." Which James continued to do, wishing he could scoop him up like Seth had done to him before.

"I need to do this, baby," he countered. "Quinn and I were best friends growing up, even though we came from vastly different families and situations. But the part you need to know is that Quinn is, was a lesbian and Danni was the child she had always wanted but needed help to have."

"Seth, love, I'm so sorry you lost her." James pulled Seth's head to his shoulder, a silent offer of support and comfort.

"Thanks, but baby, now you have both of us here," Seth began but stopped. His hand tightened around James's for a moment.

"I'm happy to have you around more, sir, and I always wanted a child. I don't mind sharing my place." James didn't like where this topic could lead.

"I had planned to introduce you to them this next weekend," Seth continued as if he had never spoken. "Quinn was excited to meet you, actually. She knew how much you meant to me and thought we should tell you together about Danni. She insisted that you would take it better if you could see that she was no threat to you, to us."

Seth took a breath and shuddered, then slowly turned in James's arms and cuddled closer. "But, now you only have my word about Danni. I wasn't trying to hide her, baby."

Before Seth could continue that train wreck of a thought, James interrupted gently. "Seth, please listen to me. All I ever need is your word, sir. Danni doesn't threaten me or us. She's a sweet, sad little girl and I hope you will allow me to help care for and cherish her. I want you here, both of you." He winced at the slight pleading tone that had slipped into his voice, but he couldn't help it.

Seth had his heart. He didn't want it back. Ever.

"SETH," Mel's deep voice cut through Seth's wandering thoughts. Ever since Quinn died in that stupid car wreck he had trouble focusing. "Are you listening to me?"

He turned to look directly at Mel. "Yes, Mel. I heard you; I simply do not know how to fix this particular problem. Not cleanly, at least."

"They have to be more creative than most, thanks to your status in the community, money, and with the fact she can't use your sexuality against you as I'm sure they are wont to do. But you are in a steady relationship," Mel hinted, the nudge quite clear to Seth, though it made the idea no less appealing.

"So, your *advice* to me is that I should propose to and marry James on the grounds that it shuts down part of Danni's grandparents' custody suit?" Seth asked, face pinched up as he rubbed his aching head. "Never mind if James would wish to marry me, if I wish to marry him, or the fact he would probably end up feeling like I was using him instead of loving him. How can you honestly support doing that to James, Mel?"

"James worships the very ground you walk on and you know it. Danni already has him wrapped around her little finger, in case you didn't notice. Oh, and you love him, whether you admit it or not."

Seth stared at Mel, dumbfounded. He knew what he felt, and James had revealed he felt the same not that long ago, but marriage? And for such a reason?

"Show how they threw Quinn out when she was seventeen for kissing another girl. Point out that they have had little to no contact with Danni and she does not know them. Hell, doesn't the fact I am on the birth certificate, pay for Danni's school and insurance, or that she is happy with us count for anything?" Seth nearly bellowed.

"Of course it does, Seth," Mel said, attempting to placate Seth's fear and anger. "But they have already contacted Zach and a few others from your past. You know what they will try to make you look like."

Seth's eyes turned deadly as he pinned Mel with his stare. "You, of all people, have no right to go there."

"*I* didn't," Mel said, his voice just as cold and hard as Seth's. "They did. Quinn's parents are looking for anything they can to make you look unfit. I can publicly tear them down, but for Danni's sake, I do *not* want to do any more damage to her grandparents than is absolutely necessary." Mel suddenly perked up, his lips curling in a devilish grin. "Besides, think how dashing James would look in a tux."

Seth groaned, pinched the bridge of his nose, and shook his head at his best friend and lawyer. "You, you're worse than Britt and your daughters combined. I swear!"

Mel's peals of laughter reverberated on the walls in the office. His mirth was so infectious that even Seth cracked a reluctant smile.

Finally Mel settled and took a more serious stance and tone again. "Seriously, Seth, think about the idea. I think you'd like being married to James," he added pointedly.

chapter fourteen

A MOTORCYCLE rumbled down the well-lit street James lived on, drawing his attention as he led Danni to the door of their home. He noted the figure that straddled the bike as it pulled up to the curb in front of them.

Once the bike stopped, the black leather clad rider stood, swung his leg over it, and rose to his rather imposing full height. James would have to tilt his head back to look the man in the face, he was sure, and at six-one himself, he found that both impressive and nerve-wracking.

The man pulled off his helmet as he looked between James and Danni. Danni's eyes brightened and a smile burst across her face. "Rhys! Uncle James, its Rhys!" she squealed and ran toward the stranger.

"Danni, you come back here right now," James snapped as he moved as fast as he could on crutches to catch up to her.

The huge man smiled down at the little girl and squatted to be closer to her level. "Danni, your friend here is right, honey. Since he doesn't know me, he's going to think I'm dangerous." The rumble of laughter as Danni pouted warmed James to the stranger, some.

"Excuse me, I realize that you two *seem* to know each other but as I don't, I'd really rather Danni come back over here. Now."

Ignoring James's worry, Danni grabbed Rhys's hand and started pulling him toward James. "Come meet Unc—Daddy's boyfriend, Rhys. He draws and paints and cooks all kinds of yummy stuff. You'll like him, promise," she explained, her words nearly running together she spoke them so fast.

Once closer Rhys released Danni's hand, removed his gloves, and offered his hand to James. "Danni's always been a little excitable," he said with a smile. "I'm sorry for just up and stopping by but Seth asked me to come over and talk to you. Could we move inside to speak?"

James noted that the entire time Rhys's eyes had roamed, as if looking for someone or something—a point that made him nervous. *Invite the hulking stranger in? With Danni? Uh, no.*

"Danni honey, please go inside. I'll be right behind you. I just need to speak with your friend for a moment," James explained. He hated to push her away but figured the simple reasoning should suffice.

She looked between James and Rhys, shrugged, took James's keys, and bounded to the door. Once she was inside, James turned back to face Rhys, who held out a cell toward him.

"I figure you're worried about who I am and that Seth forgot to call you, so here," Rhys said and waggled the phone again.

James cautiously took the cell, looking between it and Rhys, then held it to his ear. "Hello?"

"James? Sorry I did not call earlier. Meetings," he added as if that explained everything—which to James, it did. "The rather large man in front of you is Rhys Sayer, Officer Sayer's big brother. I've hired him as a sort of bodyguard for right now. He can explain everything. I need you to work with him for now. Okay, baby?" Seth asked, his voice soft and low. The tone sent a shiver down James's spine, against his wishes.

"Yes, sir. But, um, why do we need a guard?"

"Rhys can explain. Just cooperate and be good, James. I should be home a little early today. I will bring dinner, so talk and relax. I need to go, baby."

"Um, okay. Bye, love," James replied, thrilling slightly at being able to openly call Seth that. He turned to face Rhys again, uncertain of the man, but he trusted Seth. "Well, it seems I'm to invite you in and that you now work for Seth, so um, welcome. Come in," he added as he gave a thin smile and turned to head inside.

James grumbled under his breath as he headed into the house, pausing long enough to make sure his "guard" followed. He held the door for the man to enter, then closed it behind him. As he headed into the great room, searching for Danni, he noted that Rhys stopped to check and lock the front door. He continued to watch as Rhys moved to the windows before he moved to follow James.

"Window walls?" Rhys groaned. A small frown twisted his lips as he stared at the wall in the great room.

James scowled at the man. "And just what exactly is wrong with my walls? I like light," he added with a slight huff.

He ran his fingers through his dark hair, long enough to brush his collar, ruffling it as he continued to stare at the windows. Rhys turned his chin enough to be heard but not to meet James's eyes. "Seth wants you and Danni safe, sir, but anyone with a rock from your woods back there and a little determination can gain access to your home. With all these windows there is no way to really secure the house fully," he explained. "Well, short of mesh or something, bars maybe." His lips suddenly quirked up, and then he added, "Of course, it does make the room feel twice as large as it actually is, so I can't fault ya. Not from a homeowner's point of view."

"Well, thanks. I think."

James looked over Rhys, taking in the ruffled, longer hair and permanent five o'clock shadow on his rugged face before moving over his leather and denim. The look screamed sex-on-wheels, especially when he thought of how he'd looked getting off his bike. Rhys was too massive and scary for him to feel any attraction, plus he admitted—albeit silently—that all he'd craved since their first kiss in the parking garage was Seth. However, the man inspired him and he itched to go sketch and paint.

Annoyed that he'd had to listen to how his house was not good enough, he headed to the kitchen to fix Danni a light snack before he sent her to play. "When you are satisfied with inspecting in here, you may come to the kitchen. I'll even make enough for you to have some too," James offered, barely able to restrain from smirking.

By the time Rhys made it into the kitchen, Danni was settled at the counter, primly atop her favorite stool—not that James had managed to figure out what made that one special—enjoying herself.

James looked over to his visitor and smiled. "Ants on a log?" he offered.

"Um," he began. Before he could say yes or no, Danni imperiously gestured to the stool next to hers as only small children and the idle rich can manage. With a shrug, Rhys sat and answered, "Sure?"

James sat a couple of "logs" on a plate in front of Rhys, then faced Danni. "Pixie, Rhys and I need to talk so when you're done, you can play in your room or sit at the table and draw, but I don't want you wandering."

"Okay," she chirped, peanut butter smeared on the edge of her little mouth. "I want to color," she announced as she finished.

"Wash up first, please. Thank you."

James got Danni settled at the dining table with her crayons and papers, then led Rhys outside to the chairs on the stone deck. "Will this suffice? I don't want Danni to hear anything that might upset her. She's only just starting to act like a normal kid for more than half an hour at a time."

"No, this is fine," Rhys said. He sat across from James after looking around a moment. "You have a really nice house here. I didn't mean to upset you, before I mean. I'm concerned about your safety, as is Seth."

"I don't really understand. Why do we need a bodyguard, Rhys?" James asked, fidgeting in his seat slightly. He didn't like that Seth had done this without talking to him first.

"Two reasons that I know of. First, Danni's grandparents have threatened to take her from Seth, something I won't let happen.

Ever!" he snapped. After taking a deep breath to calm, he continued. "Sorry. I know some of what they put her mom through and will fight with everything I have to keep her with Seth, not them. And second—"

"Wait, you knew her mom? Danni's I mean?" James interrupted, eyes wide as he waited.

"Yeah, I knew her," he murmured and looked down, his tone sullen. "Still can't believe a stupid car wreck took her from us." Rhys stayed quiet for a few moments before looking up again to face James.

"She seems to have been a special woman. I'm sorry I never met her."

"She was."

"And second," James redirected.

"Right. And second, there was a recent threat against you. Plus, my little brother told me you had a run in with an ex a while back that landed you in the hospital. Is that why the crutches?" Rhys asked.

James knew it was a common concern to those around him, but he still hated the looks of pity they often engendered in others. "Wait. Your brother said?"

"Yeah," he said with a shrug. "He said he met you when he and his partner came over unofficially to help make sure your ex didn't get away with battery. Officer Dal Sayer?" It sounded more like a question to James than a statement.

"Officer Sayer? Oh, right. The two that came over the same time as Mel about proof of past violence…. But, I don't know why he went to you about Victor." His voice cracked on the last word. Swallowing hard, he composed himself again. "What threat?" he finally asked, though he wasn't certain he truthfully wanted to know.

"Seth just said there had been a threat against you and that he would give me more details later," he explained with a tentative look. Something about the way Rhys didn't quite look at him made him curious and irritated. "Dal only brought it up to me because I said I was heading out to a job. He said you were nice but shy, if that helps any," he added with a grin that nearly split his face.

He already knew Seth was up to something so decided to put the questions on hold, until Seth came home.

SHAKING his head at his sketch, James wished he had the courage to ask Rhys to pose for him. He especially wanted to get a peek at the tattoo he could see the barest edge of from under his shirtsleeve when the man flexed his arms. The large man across the room inspired his artistic nature, so he sat sideways on the couch, knees pulled up to make a brace for his sketch pad, as he worked out a design he thought Britt would love to add to her *Touch* show.

As he erased part of the sketch, again, he heard keys in the front door, then the door open and close.

"Hello," Seth called out.

James raised his head to peer over the top of the pad and realized Rhys stood in the foyer, blocking his view of Seth.

"Welcome home, Seth." James sighed as his heart tightened in joy at the word. "Rhys, it's just Seth.... You know, the guy you swear hired you? Relax," James teased, barely able to resist laughing at the situation.

"Yes, sir." Rhys moved to the side as Seth came into the great room.

"How was your day, sir?" James asked.

"It was a day," Seth replied, his shoulders sagged under the weight of the take-out bags he held. "Unfortunately that is about the best I can say. Now, how was your day? Are you and Rhys getting on okay?" He gave a small smile as he passed and headed into the kitchen.

James closed the sketchpad, looked over at Rhys cautiously, and headed into the kitchen to help Seth.

"I brought Italian, in case you can't tell. Where is Danni?" Seth suddenly asked, worry clearly etched into his beautiful face.

James shook his head. "Do you really think between the two of us, we could lose her? Seriously?"

"No?"

"You're obviously more tired than I thought," he murmured. James leaned out of the kitchen and called Danni to wash up and come to dinner.

All four of them sat at James's dining table, a novelty that silently pleased him greatly. He still felt strange at times, all this *having people in his house* thing. But he couldn't imagine anything better than having *his* Seth and Seth's daughter there with him.

They spent time with Danni after dinner, up until bedtime for her, while Rhys tinkered with windows and doors and installed various small cameras and sensors, set to record anyone who approached their home.

Once Danni was settled in bed—book read and water glass obtained—they all retired to the back stone patio to talk, Seth insisting that in bed for a six-year-old did not mean asleep yet.

"Okay, so would one of you, please, let me in on what's going on," James demanded, arms folded across his chest. He looked at Seth but did not care which of them answered, just that he was let in on the secret.

"Show him, Seth. I know you want to protect him, but he needs to know," Rhys insisted. He and Seth were locked in a staring contest, it seemed to James.

"Seth?" James asked softly. "Please."

Seth sighed and pulled his glower from Rhys. "James, baby, there was a threat made against you and what with the Johnsons trying to fight dirty to get Danni from me, I hired Rhys to protect you two. Before you ask," Seth cut off the questions building on James's lips, "Mel is working on derailing the attempt with Danni. They will not get her from us, don't worry."

James nodded slowly, thinking through what Seth had said. "I trust Mel to protect her, especially after him supporting me, us, through Victor's trial." He paused as the memory of that victory swamped him. Vic had lost the court battle and was now in prison for years due to felony battery charges for the attack at the bar.

Shaking off the memory, James continued. "But Seth? What threat against me? Vic's in jail and Ty would never do anything that could be traced back to him. I can't believe that Brian would come after me, though I'm sure he blames me for the firing." James continued to stare, hoping Seth would be open and honest with him.

"Knew I should have done this before you got here, Seth," Rhys grumbled. He reached into his pocket and pulled out a folded up piece of paper and handed it to James. "This is a copy of the letter Seth turned over to the police. He managed to convince them to hold off on talking to you until tomorrow because he hired me and my baby brother was one of the officers that responded to the call."

James looked at the paper, unfolded it, and smoothed it out before what was printed on it registered. The paper was a copy of a threat. Against him, specifically. It looked as if someone had cut out words from a magazine or newspaper and glued them on the page. It read:

James

Stop spreading your Filth. Stay away from children. All Fags should Die.

At the bottom was a crude drawing of someone with a knife stabbed into them surrounded by a puddle of what he supposed was originally red—blood.

chapter fifteen

JAMES startled, dropping his pencil, when he suddenly felt lips graze his bare shoulder. As the world resolved around him, he remembered where he was, leaned back against Seth's legs as he sat on the floor in the great room.

Feeling his cheeks heat, he lifted his head, tilting it to meet Seth's eyes. "Yes, sir? You need me to move?" James asked softly.

"No, baby," Seth replied, absently running his fingers through James's hair. "But your phone is ringing," he added with a quick smile.

"Oh," James mumbled. "Right." James set his sketchpad and pencils down to dig in his pocket for his cell. It had stopped ringing, but the tone had been Chase's, so he called him right back.

"Chase? What's up?"

"Ah, there you are," Chase greeted, his voice bubbly, even for him. "Guess what?"

"You know I hate that game, Chase. Wait, are you drunk?" James asked. He heard loud music in the background and wondered why Chase would call him from a club. On a Saturday night.

"Only a little, Jamie! But you need to guess. Please," Chase begged.

"Chase," James nearly growled. He hated when Chase got drunk. It usually meant he had to go out at some god-awful hour to rescue him.

"Bah, you're no fun," Chase groused. "Fine. I wanted to tell you that I just got some dirt on your little boyfriend and man, are you gonna be happy I told you before it's too late. Wait, are you alone?"

"No. Hold on." James moved to stand but Seth stopped him. Mouthing that he would go instead, he snatched up James's sketches and left him with just his phone. "Now I am. What are you blathering on about?" James snapped.

"Seth. The man's getting married! I'm assuming it's not to you or you would have told me already."

"Chase," James ground out. "Where do you get such ideas? He's with me, no matter who he may have been with before." Or he hoped that was right. *Seth moved in so surely he's not still playing with others....* "And married? To whom?" he added softer, though he wasn't certain he wanted to know. Chase was flakey at times, but he was never intentionally cruel or petty.

"I don't know but Sam"—hiccup—"he works in Seth's lawyer friend's office, said he heard Mr. Holcomb talking to Seth about marriage and legal issues. Then"—hiccup—"Sam says he saw a copy of a prenip, uh, prenup with Seth's name on it."

"Chase, you're going to string yourself up tomorrow when you sober up. Even if it was true, and I don't believe he would do that to me, calling me drunk to tell me is... I don't know what it is, but I'm hanging up now," James snapped and turned off his phone, deciding that hanging up simply wasn't enough.

Once he had set the cell aside, James stared down at his graphite-smudged hands, not really seeing anything. He couldn't help wondering if any of what Chase said was true, and if there was any hope of changing things if it were.

So lost in his circular thoughts he jumped when Seth's face suddenly appeared in front of him. "Wha—"

"James, baby, why are you crying?" Seth asked, his voice low and soothing. Before he could manage a response, James felt Seth's arms wrap around him, pulling him up and into his lap.

I'm taller than him, damn it. He shouldn't be able to manhandle me so easily, he thought and scowled.

"I'm not," James mumbled and wiped at his face, silently cursing his traitorous tears. *Damn it,* he hadn't wanted Seth to see him cry, again.

"James," Seth countered. He knew that tone; it was the *Do Not Lie To Me* tone.

James shook his head but still didn't speak. Defying Seth could be dangerous to their continued relationship, especially depending on if any of what Chase said was true, but he couldn't say it.

"Pet, hand me your cell." Seth's voice was hard and clipped. He knew he'd upset Seth but....

Reluctantly, James reached over and picked up his phone. He looked at it as if it might bite—he was certain it could—and slowly handed it to Seth. Seth took the cell, and once it was back on, called the last incoming number.

"Chase, what did you say to James?" Seth demanded into the phone. James couldn't hear Chase, though he kind of wished he could. "No, that's not true. Why would you say something like that to James?" James went still at the denial. He hoped it meant what he thought it did. "Damn it, you had better be glad you're his best friend, Chase." The anger in Seth's voice continued to build. "No, you may not come over.... Well, as James decided to move Danni and me in, it's *our* home now, so yes, I do have a say." James finally moved, torn between fear and elation at the declaration of it being *our home*. "Good-bye, Chase!" he finally bellowed, so angry that instead of hanging up or clicking off, he threw the cell, shattering it against the far wall.

James was so startled that he almost missed Danni crying out in the other room. Without forethought, James retrieved his crutches, stood, and headed toward Danni's room. He paused just before he turned the corner to look at Seth. *What the hell?* He couldn't believe Seth had done that, not even considering what had been said.

"Seth, I expect that cleaned up when I get back out here," James said, his tone low. His hands hurt from how tight he held his crutches due to his anger and fear. "We need to talk." With that last cryptic remark, he headed to Danni, hoping it was a regular nightmare and not that she had heard Seth's misbehavior.

By the time he made it back out to the great room, Seth had indeed cleaned up the broken phone and sat quietly on the couch, toying with his own cell.

Seth looked up, regret clear in his eyes. "James?"

"Do I need to worry about you hitting or throwing anything else?" *Like me?*

"No," Seth answered, not meeting James's eyes. "I didn't mean to do that. I don't want you afraid of me. Please," he added as he patted the couch next to him.

James looked him over, contemplating how to handle this. "I will sit. And yes, we are going to talk, but I will not tolerate violence, Seth. Not from anyone, but especially not from you." His hands shook slightly, but he managed to get all the words out.

"Agreed." Seth watched as James moved over and sat beside him, half turning on the couch so they could face each other. "I will get you a new phone tomorrow, baby."

"Don't, Seth. You can't buy your way out of this," James countered, barely able to restrain the growl that wanted to break free. "I swore I wouldn't let anyone hurt me again and I definitely won't let anyone hurt Danni. You can't just buy something to 'make it all better.'"

James nearly apologized for his words when he saw the stricken look on Seth's face. But, no. He had to do this.

"I didn't mean I'd buy you a phone to fix things. You need a phone and my poor behavior lost you yours," Seth explained. "And I really did not mean to do that. Chase just made me so angry. I tell Mel I won't do that to you and somehow Chase finds out and blabs but gets all the details wrong."

"What—what do you mean? What parts did he get right?" he asked, trembling at the idea of any of what Chase had said being right. He'd been so certain that Seth loved him, even if he didn't exactly say it. He showed it in so many ways.

Seth sighed and ran his fingers through his hair roughly. "Mel did suggest I marry you, but I told him no."

He had never thought about marriage, not considering his track record, but suddenly the idea that Seth would reject the suggestion caused tears to spill again and his heart to lurch painfully. God, he felt like such a child!

"No, no, baby," Seth begged. "You have it all wrong. I would love to offer you a life together, a real family, but not for the reasons Mel brought it up. Not to convince the courts I'm a stable parent or to simply protect Danni. I won't do that and I told Mel so. How that turned into me marrying someone behind your back, I have no clue."

"Wait! You would *want* to marry me at some point?"

"Er, um, well… yes," Seth mumbled, his hands twisting together nervously. "I just—"

James let out a happy whoop and suddenly landed in Seth's lap. He peppered his face in kisses while laughing, relieved that Seth wasn't leaving him for some mystery person.

"Baby, calm down," Seth laughed.

"But, that means you love me, right? And you're not leaving me," James added as he beamed at Seth.

"Yes. No! Wait, why on earth would I do that?" Seth reached out, placed his hands on either side of James's face, and feathered his lips across his beloved's. "James, I love you. I would never have moved in with you and let Danni get attached to you if I didn't. I thought you would understand that even though I had never said the words quite so blatantly."

"Well, he mentioned prenups and marriage and well, he said Sam from Mel's office is who told him so…."

"I will deal with Sam and Mel tomorrow. For now, please believe that you are loved, wanted, and my only." Seth pulled him to his chest for a moment. When he pulled back, he frowned. "Baby, why are you crying now? I though you would be happy."

"I am, love. These are happy tears. Promise," James explained as he leaned in to seal his mouth over Seth's. He still trembled from the revelation that his Seth loved him.

SETH grasped James's chin and pulled him into a soft kiss. James responded eagerly, trying to deepen the kiss, but he held James steady, controlling where the kiss went. James tugged at Seth until he could shift to straddle his lap.

Seth allowed James to manhandle him, reveling in the passion and love he felt radiating off his lover. He didn't want to do anything that might worry or frighten James. He let his hands slide up James's arms, then down his sides until he could shift James back a little. "Pet, bedroom, now," he panted between kisses.

James groaned. "Right, Danni," he all but whined. "Hurry up, then, please. I need you, sir." It took only a few moments for them to get into their bedroom and shed all clothing.

Before James could do more than sit on the edge of the bed, Seth stretched and moved him until he was in the center of it. All the rush seemed to go out of Seth as he took in the kiss-swollen lips and half-lidded hungry gaze of the man before him. The man he wanted to make his, in all ways. Leaning in, he again took James's lips, but in a slow, achingly tender display that left them both shaken and in awe.

It was forever yet not nearly long enough when Seth pulled back again. He reached out to trace James's lips with his fingers, completely overcome with desire and tenderness—an odd combination in his experience.

"What do you want, baby," Seth inquired, dragging his eyes back up to meet James's.

"You, only you."

He moved his body to settle between James's legs, then rolled his hips to grind their cocks together. "The things you say," Seth said, diving in to take James's lips in a demanding kiss. He felt more than heard the rumble of James's moan as he took what was his.

He could feel how James's body reacted to him as he kissed lightly down his neck and chest to lick and nibble on the tiny bud. He reveled in how James moaned and squirmed as he continued to lavish attention on his nipples and rock their bodies together.

He continued his sensual assault of James's senses as he slowly slithered his way down his body until he was even with James's weeping cock. Seth leaned in to swipe his tongue across the head, lapping up the musky, viscous pearls seeping from the slit. James cried out and moved his legs wider apart as he begged for Seth to either suck him or fuck him; he didn't seem to care which.

Seth chuckled and nuzzled James's sack before he pushed his legs up and flicked his tongue down James's taint to finally swipe across the tight, fluttering pucker there. He worked his tongue in alternating stabs, licks, and swirls to open James up before he slowly added first one finger, then another.

James writhed and rocked against Seth's fingers, begging him to please fill him before he died. "Please," he keened.

"Oh, I'm going to fill you, alright, but pet," Seth said as he twisted his fingers hard inside James. "Listen to me, baby. I'm going to fuck you, but you are not allowed to come. Understand?"

James let out a desperate cry but nodded obediently.

Once he had James's agreement, Seth quickly sheathed his cock and lined himself up. He used his thumbs to open James as he slowly pushed inside, reveling in the sounds coming from his lover as he took everything James could give him.

James gripped the sheets tightly as his thrusts became harder, deeper. Seth felt James wrap his legs around his hips and arch up, obviously trying to get some stimulation on his own cock. Seth shifted angles to keep James from succeeding, amused at the disgruntled growl James let out.

His strokes sped up as his rhythm faltered just before he lost his battle and came deep inside James, the sheer pleasure whiting out his vision for a short time. As the world came back into focus around him, he leaned down to capture James's lips in another scorching kiss before he slowly pulled out, careful of the condom.

He shifted back and took in the quivering body stretched out before him. After a moment, Seth reached out, producing a second condom, which he quickly opened and rolled down James's twitching cock.

"Seth?" James asked, confusion and frustration clear in his lust-hazed eyes. No answer came. Seth simply climbed up James's body, kissing and nibbling as he went until he was seated against James's groin.

Seth drew in a deep breath as he lifted, reached back, and grasped James's cock before he began to slowly sink down onto it. His eyes closed at the pleasure-pain that ripped through him as James stretched and filled him. Even though he had just come, he had to remind himself not to get too wild or loud as James began his slow and sensual thrusts up, moving inside him wordlessly as he levered himself up and down to meet the overpowering pleasure that only joining their bodies together could produce in him.

He gasped wordlessly as James increased the speed and started slamming up into him. The sounds James made as he continued to thrust mixed with the desperate way he clawed at his back had Seth half-hard and writhing before James trembled, slamming deeper and deeper up once, twice, and one final time before Seth felt James's cock twitching inside him as he came, finishing inside him just as he had in his James.

Seth rolled his hips to draw out the pleasure for them until James whimpered below him softly and pulled free with a plaintive gasp.

"I—I can't believe you did that again, love," James said with a sigh.

Seth lowered himself slowly to the bed and gently curled around James, relishing the aches he felt now and oddly looking forward to the ones he would have tomorrow. "Did what, pet?"

James stretched in his arms and shook his head. "Shared yourself with me like that, sir. Every time I think I have you figured out, you do something like this," James explained as he snuggled deeper in Seth's arms.

"What? You don't like when I bottom from the top?" He laughed at the incredulous look on James's face.

"No, I love that, though I never expected to do such a thing. I just—no one… I don't know how to explain it, Seth."

"Relax, baby. I understand. You never expected to be the giver, it's okay."

"That, yes. But, um, thank you for sharing your body with me," James added so softly Seth nearly missed it.

"Oh, my love. That is something you never need say thank you for," he explained and kissed James tenderly. "I love you, James."

"And I, you. But—" James paused. He nibbled his bottom lip a moment before he asked, "Seth? Did you really mean what you said?"

As he looked into James's eyes, Seth could see the love and desire there. He also saw the worry buried deep inside. His beloved feared he would leave still, *ridiculous.*

Finally Seth reached out, lacing their fingers together, and kissed his gently. He squeezed James's hand as he put their joined hands over his heart, and whispered against James's ear, "You are mine, James, just as I am yours. Always."

James sniffed as he nodded against Seth's cheek.

Twisting their bodies together, Seth wondered if James would ever truly believe him, that he honestly did love and desperately want him. "Sleep, baby. I've got you. Forever," he offered quietly as he felt James drift off.

chapter sixteen

JAMES and Chase sat together on the couch in the great room of James's stone cottage for the longest time. His best friend listened to everything he'd said about proposals, anger, the phone, even the apology and explanation—he only left out the part about the sex, and how special he thought it was. But Chase remained skeptical of "Seth's intentions," as he put it.

He understood where Chase was coming from, but he simply could not believe that Seth was lying or using him. James offered to take him and Danni in; Seth had never asked. He gave him a key to the house before that, Seth hadn't asked for one. Arguing with Mel over marriage, considering the reasons given, made sense to him. And Seth was right, he would have wondered if Seth really even wanted him or if he was just a means to an end. *Not a way to feel or live*, in James's opinion.

So there they were, Chase on the couch, situated at the end, James lying with his head in Chase's lap as they talked. Seth would be home soon, but Britt had asked if she could have Danni sleep over. At least he didn't have to worry about anything they said being overheard. Of course, he figured Seth had probably put Britt up to it, but appreciated it nonetheless. He needed to talk things out with Seth, but had gotten a little sidetracked the night before. *In a good way*. He felt his cheeks warm slightly. *But sex couldn't fix things, just delay them*, he reminded himself.

"What are you thinkin' about that's got your face so red, huh?" Chase asked with a leer.

"Nothing."

"Okay, now pull the other one," Chase quipped.

James knew better than to continue to dodge—it *never* worked with him. "Just thinking about last night, but before you ask, no, I will not tell you anything! So quit. Right now I need to focus on what happened before bed last night and just before you got here today."

Chase's face sobered at the reminder, *sort of*.

"Jamie, are you sure you want to do this whole 'Having it out' thing with me still here?" Chase asked as he absentmindedly continued to play with James's hair. "I don't mind but…." He trailed off, right eyebrow arched and a mischievous grin in place.

"Yes. I don't want to think I could be wrong about Seth, but—"

"But you have sucky taste in men and last night scared you?" Chase asked softly.

"This morning wasn't any better, but I need to focus on Seth before stalkers."

Before Chase could respond, they heard the front door open and then close quietly. James knew it could only be Seth or Rhys, but he hadn't heard the bike. He looked toward the foyer, still laid out across the couch, as Seth came into view.

He held a small bag from the cell store in one hand. Across his normally sure and powerful features was an unaccustomed frown. He could clearly see the worry in Seth's beautiful ever-changing hazel eyes.

"Hi, baby," Seth said as he approached the couch. He paused as James sat up and made room for him to sit. He then looked over to Chase and added, "Hello, Chase."

"Hey, Seth. I'm not here to cause trouble, but seriously? I know I screwed up last night but throwing things?" Chase asked with his head tilted, his tone snarky.

James reached over and playfully smacked the back of Chase's head. "Shut up, you twit. If you hadn't called, drunk I might add, and run off at the mouth without verifying anything first, none of this would be happening."

He watched Chase rub the spot and smiled. When Chase scowled, he added, "You so deserved that, and you know it!"

"Eh, probably but that doesn't excuse Mr. Break-Things-That-Aren't-His and his little temper tantrum," Chase added with a pout.

James started to snark back, but Seth interrupted him. "James," he said softly and held up the bag he had entered the room with.

James stopped, looked from the bag to Seth, then snapped his mouth shut. "Um, thanks, I think." He carefully took the bag and looked inside to see what Seth had gotten him to replace the now busted cell. What he found was a top-of-the-line smartphone, a carry case for it, and a new Bluetooth.

"Oh, cool, James. He got you pretties," Chase teased and leaned over James to try to snatch the phone from his hands.

James smacked the grasping hands. "Hey, those are mine, brat. Seriously, Seth, you didn't need to do all this. You only broke the phone, not the Bluetooth and this cost too much."

"James, stop. I shouldn't have broken yours but I also know that you wanted this phone, so it worked out in your favor. But—"

"But we need to discuss last night," James finished. He set aside the bag and its goodies. He took a deep breath before he mustered the courage to raise his eyes to meet Seth's, more worried about what Seth would see in his than what he would find in Seth's.

"I know it doesn't excuse my behavior but between your tears and Chase's attitude," Seth explained. He looked past James to Chase to continue. "Do you even remember what you said to me last night? Or understand the condition I found your so-called best friend in?"

"Chill," Chase snapped. "I know I screwed up, but that's between Jamie and me. You need to fix what you did." Chase sat back, arms crossed, as he looked at Seth and continued, "I pissed him off but you, you have the power to destroy him. I'm not going to just sit here and let that happen. I made a mistake last night and called to warn him about something that I believed was wrong, but the intention was good. He's already done his yelling at me. You don't get that privilege, yet."

"But over the phone? Drunk."

"Psh," Chase said as he waved off the comment. "Throwing things. Breaking things. With a kid in the house, even? Hmm?" Chase countered.

James fought to not smile as he watched the two most important men in his life bicker over who had more to answer for due to the previous night's stupidity. Seth opened his mouth to reply to Chase, but James placed his hand softly against Seth's lips to hold the words back. "He already said he was sorry and promised never to drunk call for anything but a ride in the future. Okay?"

Seth nodded but let James keep his fingers against his lips. "Good. Now, do I need to worry about your outburst?"

Seth lifted his hand up to gently move James's, twining their fingers together as he spoke. "No, baby. I know to you that probably seemed out of line but the tears and fear in your eyes…. It wasn't you I was mad at, and while I thought about throttling your friend here, I would never actually do that." They smiled at each other when Chase let out a low *harrumph.* "I was also upset that this came out of Mel's office. I had already given him my *no* but that didn't stop the damage.

"Oh, and Chase," Seth added, though his eyes never left James's. "For all you knew, you could have messed up an attempt to get things in order for an actual proposal. Did it even cross your mind that if I was to get married, it would be to James, not some random mystery man?"

"I—um, no. Oh man! Were you going to propose to James? Please tell me I didn't really screw that up for him," Chase ranted. James and Seth had already discussed this, but watching Chase squirm was almost too much for James.

"No, and we already talked that out as well," he explained before again addressing James.

"But, baby, why were you lying down in Chase's lap? Your eyes look a little swollen," Seth added and gently touched James's face just below his right eye.

"I don't want to talk about it," he replied and turned his head away from Seth's touch.

"No, something is obviously wrong if you are trying to hide your face from me. What else happened? And where's Rhys?" Seth asked, looking around suddenly.

Chase reached out and patted James's arm. "I got this one, hun. Seth, he got another threat, but this one's a bit different. I didn't meet this Rhys person, he left just before I got here, but I know your guy's partner is outside somewhere."

As he continued to explain, Chase pulled out his cell and started tapping the screen. After a moment he handed it to Seth. He wrapped his arms around James and pulled him back against him as Seth looked at the image. Giving a squeeze to James, Chase continued, "James had Rhys text me a picture of the threat. I'm assuming he didn't send you one, or you'd know already, but um, Seth? Is your guard friend enough to protect Jamie?" he added, his voice slightly higher and faster than normal.

James watched as Seth stared at the little screen. He wanted Seth to say it would be alright, but he was too nervous to speak right then. Too many negatives running through his head: *What if this is simply too much to deal with? Would he take Danni and leave for their safety? Will he leave me now?*

Seth's face twisted in a deep scowl as he looked from the cell to James and back. "Where is this photo from?" he thundered. "When did you ever look like this and by whose hand?"

Before James or Chase could answer, Seth was up, pacing the great room in long jerky steps. Voice so soft he was surprised Seth heard him, James replied, "Um, that's part of why Rhys left, sir. That's a police photo from the first time 911 was called in after the 'accident.' The only people to have that picture would be the police and maybe the lawyers from the case."

"What about in all that stuff you gave Mel a couple months ago? He didn't let me look through the files, something about client confidentiality," Seth added with a grunt.

"No. Not this one. I don't know how someone got it but, um," James paused, not meeting Seth's eyes as he chewed on the side of his mouth.

"Um, what, pet?" Seth said, his voice obviously strained but controlled.

"Did you read the caption, yet?"

Seth closed his eyes tight for a moment, then opened and fidgeted with the cell again.

All Faggs Should Die!

Stay away from descent people & children or this will be nothing compared to what will happen!

Die pervert!!!

"But it's Sunday. How was this delivered?" Seth mumbled. "Never mind."

He pulled out his phone and started dialing. "Rhys? Yeah, what is going on and why is James unprotected?" Seth demanded into the cell. Seth continued to pace while he ranted at Rhys. The worry lines between his eyes and across his forehead seemed to etch deeper the longer he talked. He nearly wore out a path from the great room to the front windows before he finally ended the call.

James knew his eyes swam with unshed tears, but he feared what Seth would decide. If he was really a target for some radical homophobe, it wasn't safe for Danni to be around him or his home. It broke his heart to think of giving up the little family that had dropped on him. He loved Seth and was quickly falling for the little pixie that he read to and tucked in every night. He knew it hadn't been long but dammit, he did not want to lose them! Either of them.

They sat together for a long time, James wrapped in Seth's arms as they talked and waited for Rhys and his brother Dal Sayer, the cop, to arrive at the house. They had managed to placate Seth about Rhys leaving by showing him that there was someone outside from Rhys's security and that there was a uniform watching the house while he was gone—though neither James nor Chase knew how he'd managed to pull that off.

James heard Rhys's motorcycle pull up outside at the same moment he was sure Seth had lost his mind.

"With everything that's happened and the threats, do you think we should at least call your folks, James? I know you are not close, but they should know about the threats, at least."

Twin incredulous looks pinned him to the couch. "Are you serious?" James asked at the same time Chase asked, "Are you nuts?"

"But they're his family. They are your family, baby. What?" he added defensively when both men continued to look at him with worried glances—the kind given when you aren't sure if the person is crazy or possibly suffering dementia, because they obviously aren't in the same reality you are.

"Why on earth would they care, Seth? They didn't when I was hurt before. *Any* of the times before," James added, his voice rising with a slight maniacal ring all of a sudden. "Rape. Beatings. Hell, they didn't even visit when I was in ICU after Victor attacked me while I was driving. It was raining but he still thought it was a good idea to hit the driver. He walked away with minimal injury. I was in a coma for two weeks, ICU for five days more after that, and in the hospital for what, a month total? That's not even discussing wheelchair or therapy time. Not once did they call, visit, or send a card. So why? *Why* the hell would I call and tell them some psycho agrees with them? That I really am just a sick pervert who never should have existed!"

"James," Chase whispered.

"I didn't mean to say all that. Oh God," James groaned. He clasped his hand over his mouth, mortified at what he'd just revealed to Seth. Chase had been the only person to know the level of his parents' hatred and disappointment in him. *At least I didn't*

144

tell him that my father even tells people he only has one son, he added mentally.

Seth sat in stunned silence as he stared blankly at James, seemingly unsure of how to respond to what he had revealed.

Chase glowered over James's shoulder at Seth and tipped his head, motioning toward James. Seth reached out, slowly, to pull James into his arms. "I didn't know, baby. I am so sorry for bringing them up, but James," Seth said, his voice soft but sure. "You do have a family, one that loves you very much," he added.

"No, I have a—friends," James corrected, leaving Seth to wonder what he had originally intended to say. "Some I even let close to me. And I have a lover that has a daughter to think about. But my family, the people who should be there no matter what, can't see who I actually am. They are too busy hating the gender of whom I love, Seth."

"No baby, you have a family. Chase, Danni, me," he added, brow arched, daring James to argue the definition of family he set forth. "Probably others if you would let people get close to you." He held up a hand to stall the argument he could see James formulating. "Yes, you have reasons to not trust, but you still build walls around yourself that block the very people who would be there for you, if you'd only allow."

"Seth," James said, but then they all heard a knock on the door. "Never mind. Rhys is back so we can focus on the current hate instead of my past."

"Look Seth, I'll go let your guard and cop in. You two figure out how you want to deal with the threat right now. And Seth," Chase added softly. "Don't push him on his bio-tards. They're even worse than he said." With that confusing statement, Chase turned and headed to the front door.

chapter seventeen

RHYS entered the great room first, followed by Dal and Chase. James had seen that look on Chase's face before and had to work hard not to grin. He knew the topic at hand was not a pleasant one, but the mingled look of lust and fear on Chase's face was wonderful to see again. He knew how rarely someone actually got to Chase, almost never, but it looked to him like Rhys might just be a possibility. *Thought so.*

No one else seemed to notice the wide-eyed look Chase shot James before he cleared his throat and practically ran to the kitchen, claiming he needed to get drinks for everyone.

"That was Chase, if you're wondering," James said and gestured to the fleeing form of his best friend. "And you both know Seth Burns already."

Now that Chase no longer distracted him, he took in Officer Dal Sayer and nearly swallowed his tongue. Dressed like Rhys instead of in his uniform, Dal stood before him with his leather jacket in hand, a tight red T-shirt on with body-hugging jeans and chunky black leather boots. Add in the wide leather bands at his wrists, the shoulder holster, and the tattoo peeking out from under his shirtsleeve—just like on Rhys—and you had a somewhat smaller version of intimidating maleness. He hadn't realized how alike they were. Dal was shorter by a couple of inches, and his muscles were less bulk, more tone, though.

"Rhys. Officer Sayer. Welcome to my home."

"I'm not in uniform, Mr. Bryant, so no need for *officer*. Just call me Dal, please. May we sit?" Dal asked, gesturing to a couple of chairs in the room.

"Of course," James said with a nod. "But, if you're Dal, shouldn't I be James?"

Dal smiled and gave a sharp nod.

Once they were seated, Seth spoke. "I don't like that you left James here, Rhys. You are supposed to guard him, not run off when something happens." His voice was cold, angry, and James was glad it wasn't aimed at him.

"You hired me to protect James and Danni," Rhys countered and scowled. "I was doing just that. Mark is outside, keeping anyone not authorized to be here *away*. I would not have left James and his friend unprotected, and you know it!"

Seth seemed to think for a moment, looked out the back window, then nodded.

"Now, to address the *actual* issues. Not long after you left, the neighbor woman from across the street stopped by with a letter for James. She said it was in her mail by mistake and wanted to return it. She was dressed up and in a hurry but insisted that I take him the mail if I wasn't going to let her do it herself. She left muttering about bossy men and mailmen that can't read."

"That's Mrs. Jazz. She's very," James paused to think about how to describe her. "She's a very driven woman. Be glad she decided you were a respectable person, Rhys. She is a serious handful if she's on a crusade," he added with a chuckle.

"Crusade? Is it possible she, this Mrs. Jazz, is in on the threats?" Dal asked.

"No. She sits on the board for the new GLBTQ Teen Center that opened about a year back. Her twin sister is a lesbian and so she decided to sponsor, support, push for, et cetera, anything promoting equality and support for those like us. Well, other than the good officer here, anyway," James added. Seth had mentioned Rhys was gay but as far as he knew, Dal was straight.

Seth and Rhys looked toward the front of the house as if they could see over to the Jazz house. "That was Cynthia Jazz?" Rhys asked.

"It was. Let her know you're a gay man and a bodyguard-slash-investigator and she's likely to hit you up for mentoring at the shelter."

"That's great to know, but can we get back to the threat and deal with donations later?" Seth snapped. "What took so long?"

"Sorry, sir," James murmured.

"What took so long," Dal explained, seemingly unaffected by Seth's irritation, "was researching the details of the case the threat photo was from. The only officer on record as having accessed your materials, other than the recent case—the one where Mr. d'Leone was finally convicted of felony battery—is an Officer Delanco. I've got someone looking into why he would have been in your case file."

James paled and audibly swallowed before he spoke. "Mike Delanco?" James's voice thinned and cracked on the name. Three heads turned to look at him, and he was certain Chase was probably staring at him from behind.

"Yes," Dal and Rhys said together.

James started shaking his head. He could see and feel the tremble in his hands as he fought the sudden rush of memories he'd hoped never to suffer through again. Before he could descend into a full-blown panic attack, he felt two sets of hands on him. He stiffened at the touches but quickly realized it was Chase and Seth trying to comfort him.

"What the hell," Rhys thundered.

"Mike was one of Ty's *sharing* buddies back in the days that James still lived at home," Chase said, staring daggers at the men. "He's a cop now?"

Dal nodded, his face pinched with worry.

"Figures a rapist would get himself into a position of power over others," Chase growled.

"That's a pretty serious accusation to level, Mr. Manning." Dal's voice was cold and tight.

"It's a fact!" Chase snapped. "Ty abused James when he was still in high school. If James didn't do, and I mean that literally, anything and anyone Ty told him to, he'd beat and rape him or hold him down so the buddy could. Athletes, mostly football, versus an artist whose joints dislocate if you handle him too harshly.... Who do you think won? Huh?"

James wanted to ask them to stop talking about him like he wasn't there, but couldn't seem to find his voice, so instead he continued to watch and listen in a detached fog. On some level, he knew Seth and Chase would be worried that he'd phased out again, but nothingness was better than hell.

Dal's mouth gaped open, but he said nothing. It was clear he had no idea the kind of person he worked with or the history of the person he was attempting to defend.

"No formal accusation was made. He would have never made it into the academy otherwise."

"True, but that was because James never went to the cops. He asked his family for help and they turned on him. Why would he have trusted the cops when he couldn't trust his own mother or brother?" Chase spat out. "You have any idea how hard it was for me and some of our college buddies to convince James to go to the police when Vic hurt him? Or how long it had been going on before he ever spoke up?"

That seemed to jar James out of his stupor. "Chase," James snapped. "They don't need to hear all that and it was ages ago."

"No. If what he said is true," Dal paused, staring at James until he gave a slow nod. "Then it's important we know. Doing background checks on Mike wouldn't do any good if you never reported anything. It would just lead us to the fact he was a friend of your brother's. But what would Mike have to do with threats against you, if it was him who took the photo?" he added in a soft mumble.

Seth looked between James, Chase, and Dal before he looked over to Rhys. "Is it possible that the threats are coming from James's own brother and friends? And if so, why?"

"I can't believe that, Seth. My brother wrote me off the moment I escaped home. He has never bothered with me in all this time. Why would he now?" James knew his voice bordered on begging, but he couldn't imagine why his own brother, so many years later, would threaten him.

"I don't know, baby," Seth answered. "But we need to look at all possibilities. Maybe Ty is the one actually behind this. He was pissed when I had him thrown out of the restaurant after he tried to force you to leave with him."

"Does Ty have a last name?" Rhys asked.

"His name is Tyler Webbs. He doesn't live locally, though. He was only in town for a convention, so I doubt it's him," James answered.

"I might agree," Rhys said. "But, he is the only link we know of between you and the only person on record as having accessed the case that photo came from. I know it's frustrating, James, but let us do our job. That's not to say we don't want any information you have, but your brother is local so it could still be any of them. They are all friends after all."

Chase bristled at Rhys's words. "Has anyone thought that the actual target might be Seth, not James?" he snapped, glowering between the brothers. "I mean, sure James has had trouble with guys attacking him, but that's always been a physical thing with someone he was involved with." At James's huff, he amended, "Even if he was not willingly involved. Happy?"

"Sorta," James replied but gave a small smile.

Seth stilled, then looked at Chase. "You think I have something to do with the threats against him?" His brows drew up, voice confused.

"Yes and no. I think it's awfully strange that James has never been the target of death threats before and now the latest threat mentions him being around kids. Your daughter is the only kid who he's really around, right?"

"Well, yes."

"Right, so what if the threat is from the grandparents, not Jamie's ex?"

"I, um," Seth mumbled. He faced Rhys again. "Is it possible that they could have this Officer Delanco in their pocket? I mean, I knew they were desperate to find a way to cause trouble so they could get Danni from me but—" He paused again to think. "It's too risky for them to do something like this," Seth finally concluded.

"Not if they don't know you have an in with the cops," Dal countered. "With your status and wealth, many would assume you would rather not risk your reputation—especially with the custody case looming. There are also many who assume that love between men can't be real or binding like het love. So, threaten your lover, get you to dump him, move back into your condo or whatever, and then it's you alone and they can try to claim that you bounce from man to man and that you drag your poor, already heartsick child into unhealthy, short-term relationships."

"That's vile!" Seth snapped, disgust dripping from his words.

"I agree but I've seen it happen."

Chase's eyes widened. "Oh, Seth. Think of it like a corporate takeover. I mean, you're a CEO and all.... You find ways to put pressure on the competition, to unbalance them in negotiations to get what you want, right?"

"Not me personally, but yes, that is what happens usually. Sometimes other companies even get dirty to get what... they... want...." Seth's voice trailed off, his eyes wide.

"So then the threats aren't real?" James asked, a desperate tinge to his words.

"While what Chase and Seth are discussing is possible, don't assume they are right or that the danger isn't real...."

IT HAD been one hell of a day—*Okay, the last 48 hours sucked.* Between the drama of the previous evening and the threat, visit, and everything that went with it, James was exhausted. He wished he could go paint, or maybe take a nap, but he knew Danni would be home shortly with Britt. They were only stopping for a few minutes as it was slumber-party-night at Britt's, but he still wanted to be available. Plus it was dinnertime, so where was he? In the kitchen cooking for his lover. Not that he minded. Not at all. He loved cooking, especially for Seth.

"Unca James?" Danni called as she bounded into the kitchen, startling him.

James put down the spoon he was using to stir the sauce on the stove, moved the pan to an empty burner, and turned to face her. "Yes, my little pixie? Are you having fun with Aunt Britt?" he asked with a smile. He didn't want to share his fear or stress with her; she was only six.

"Uh-huh," she squeaked and nodded her head in quick, tight movements. "But, um... Aunt Britt and Unc—Daddy are outside fighting. He sent me inside, like I'm too little to know they're fightin'," she added with a pout on her adorable little face.

James started to smile at the face she was making when her words managed to sink in. *Fighting*? "What do you mean, sweetie? Daddy and Britt are friends, so it can't be all that bad."

"Harrumph!" Danni crossed her little arms. "She called him a... coward." She nodded to herself as if pleased to use the last word. "But, Unca James, Daddy's not like that. He's not scared of anything." Her matter-of-fact tone and confidence in Seth warmed his heart even as his curiosity and nerves were piqued.

"Okay, pixie. How about I go find out what they're up to and you go grab your things to take back to Aunt Britt's?" James smiled as he sent Danni off to her bedroom. *Now, what are those two doing arguing in front of Danni? Really!*

James made it to the foyer before he could hear Seth and Brittany, and yes, they were arguing.

"I cannot believe you would do this to me, Britt! You know how much stress he's already under, but no, you decide that helping Mother set up a surprise visit was the right thing to do. And worse,

James is in there cooking dinner for me. You know they will expect us to go out somewhere. They probably already have reservations."

Seth's deep smooth voice was agitated in a way James had never heard before, not even earlier when they discussed the threats and the theories about who it might be. James froze at the thought of meeting Seth's parents. He knew they spoke on the phone often. Seth always seemed pleased after their talks, so he didn't figure it would be too unreasonable to think they might want to visit. But now? And with no warning?

James closed his eyes as he fought to control his breathing. No way would Seth's affluent, jet set parents want him as their son's partner. He was just an artist, not even a famous one. He reminded himself that Seth said they accepted his being gay back in high school and never showed anything but pride in him and his life. He knew he was jaded thanks to his own family, or those that were *supposed* to be his family. *But still....*

James went to turn and head back in, unsure of how to address what he'd heard, when the front door flew open and Seth stomped inside. "I am still not amused with you, Britt." Seth paused and looked at James with wide eyes, shock clear on his handsome face. "James? How long have you been standing there, pet?"

"Long enough to know your folks are on their way here and that you're probably going out with them." James looked down, not sure what else to say.

"Yes, so I just heard," Seth replied, his voice sour. "But, baby, don't worry. I'm sure Mother and Father will adore you." He raised his head and sniffed. "What are you making, by the way? It smells wonderful."

"You are not going to distract me that easily, sir."

Seth smirked and drew James into his arms. "Are you sure I can't distract you, baby?" Seth asked as he slid his hands around James's waist and pulled him closer.

"Well—"

A man cleared his throat, drawing both men's attention. James went to step back, but Seth held him a little tighter. When he looked over Seth's shoulder James saw a man that could only be Seth's father, or maybe older brother. He was an older version of his lover at the least. He had blue eyes instead of the sparking hazel of his lover's, with silver at his temples, but Seth was still the spitting image of the man taking up his doorway.

Seth turned without releasing James, and faced the man. "Hello, Father."

"Hello," the man said, a small smile on his face.

Seth's father stumbled forward a step or two, and suddenly there was a luminous, petite woman standing beside him. She was maybe five-one—if—in a white pantsuit with low heels and pearls, and a huge grin. "Seth, sweetheart!" she squealed and launched herself at her son.

chapter eighteen

"MOTHER. Father. What brings you by?" Seth asked, his arms now full of his petite mother. "If I had known you were visiting, I would have had things prepared for you."

"Oh, shush. We wanted to surprise you." James had to fight to hold back the chuckle threatening to fall from his lips as he watched his strong, confident boyfriend be scolded by his mom. "We waited a little while to give you time with Danni before we came to visit, but we wanted to meet your new man and see how you and our grandbaby are doing," she gushed, pulling him down to give him a proper hug.

Once she released Seth, she turned her attention to him. James had no choice but to pull his hand from Seth's when his mother flung herself into his arms. James knew better than to try to escape. She looked him up and down. "Introductions, please, pet," she demanded, her voice calm yet firm.

"Just a minute, Mother," Seth replied as his father stepped in to give a hug of his own.

"Mother, Father, this is my partner, James Bryant. James, this is Terra and Scott Burns."

"And I'm Danni Christine Burns," Danni chimed in as she barreled into the room and curtsied.

"Sweetheart," Terra said. "We know who you are, it's your…." She drew the word out, seemingly unsure what to say, and glanced to Seth with earnest eyes.

"Danni, you know Mimi and Pop already. They've never met your Uncle James before."

"So, they didn't come to see me too?" she asked. She batted her eyes and twisted back and forth where she stood as she peered up at Seth through her long curled lashes.

"Of course we did, baby girl," Scott boomed. He moved over and scooped her up.

"Welcome to our home, Mrs. Burns, Mr. Burns. I wasn't expecting company. I'm sorry," James added as he looked down at his jeans with the tattered knees and his lack of footwear.

"Oh, pish. We didn't fly all the way from Dublin just to inspect your clothes, James."

"Thank you. Please, come in." He motioned them all into the great room. Though still nervous, he liked Terra already—her accent charming him almost as much as her warm smile—and anyone who could make Danni happy was good with him.

After James served drinks and Seth walked Britt and Danni out, Scott spoke up. "I know we caught you just before dinner but I have to ask, what is that you made? It smells wonderful."

James beamed at the compliment. "Thank you, sir. It's shrimp with rice and veggies. That's all. I just finished the sauce when Danni came in."

"James, stop being modest."

James felt his face heat at Seth's words. "Yes, sir. Um, it's shrimp and veggie kabobs with an herbed red pepper and portabello sauce with dilled rice and roasted asparagus. I have enough for everyone, if you'd like to join us," he added.

"Sounds wonderful," Terra answered.

"You are so cute when you blush, baby," Seth whispered.

Before long they'd finished the meal. James found Seth's parents to be pleasant and, thankfully, open-minded. He started to clear the table when he felt Seth's hand on his shoulder. "Let me, James. You try to do too much."

James turned to Seth, uncertain of sitting while he worked. "But—"

Seth massaged James's shoulders for a minute and pecked his cheek as he passed and began collecting dishes. James leaned his elbows on the now clear table and gazed at Seth's powerful back as he moved around the kitchen, *their* kitchen.

His thoughts were interrupted by Terra's dainty pat on his hand. "James, dear, how do you like having Seth and Danni here?"

His brows scrunched up as he looked away from Seth to meet her eyes. "They're my family now, ma'am" was his only answer.

"Yes, yes, of course. But Seth could get a larger place for the three of you, one with a maid maybe, if you wanted."

"Mother." Seth's voice held a note of warning and annoyance.

"It's okay, Seth. No, ma'am. I have a cleaning service that comes in to help some and Seth helps as you can see. Danni's not really a messy child. Besides…." James's voice trailed off for a moment. When he did speak again, it was softer but certain. "I like having them with me. I don't wish them to move."

"I didn't mean without you, pet. I would never try to break up my son's home. We haven't seen him this happy in ages. Have we, Scott?"

"No, but I have to agree with the boys. If they're happy, leave well enough alone, Terra. They have enough going on right now; they don't need your nit-picking. Speaking of which"—Scott turned to face Seth again—"I'd like to talk with you about custody issues and support."

"Understood. We could retire to the veranda with our drinks or the great room."

"You don't have a den or study?" Scott asked with a raised brow.

"No."

"Th-that would be my fault, sir. If you want, you can use my office. I haven't had the time yet to have the spare room redone for Seth."

"Oh, baby. Don't let dad get to you. And you," Seth continued as he turned to his father, "need to back off a little too. James and I discussed it, but I don't feel right giving up our only spare room, simply for me to have a private den. Now, if you want to discuss things, pick your area and we can head out. Will you be joining us, Mother?"

"Actually, I wish to see if your James will show me some of his art. Brittany simply raves about how wonderful his work is."

James's head snapped up, his eyes wide and pleading as he stared at Seth. Friends, strangers, coworkers even, seeing his art was fine, but to show Seth's mom? "Uh…."

"It's okay, baby. She knows what kind of art you do. She's seen pictures of the ones I bought from you."

"She, she has?"

"I have, and I would like to see more. Those two are going to go into battle mode, something neither of us need be in the middle of. And before you ask, no, I do not think it's not your business or that you are too weak to participate. I know my husband and my son, though, and we would only be in the way. Now," Terra continued as she handed James his crutches, "may I see your studio?"

James accepted his sticks. He looked from Terra to Seth again, hoping for some kind of clue on what to do. Seth stood there snickering behind his hand. Scott's lips were pressed into a flat line, but even James could see the twinkle in his eyes and the twitch in his cheeks as he fought not to join Seth in his amusement.

"Oh, please, dear. It couldn't be any more pornographic than a visit to your local museum. I mean all those statues *are* anatomically correct, after all. Now, where is your art?"

JAMES'S gaze skimmed over Seth's body as he admired the smooth skin and firm, powerful muscles. When his gaze lingered over Seth's groin area, Seth growled as he licked his lips. God he wanted

Seth's cock in his mouth again, but Seth allowed him that particular delight often enough, in his opinion.

Seth reached out for the bathing sponge and shower gel when James's hand shot out. "Please, let me, sir." He waited, nibbling on his bottom lip, and hoped Seth would say *yes*.

Seth shook his head, a wicked grin spread across his face. "Grab the showerhead and don't move or come until I tell you to."

James swallowed hard but nodded and raised his hands to wrap them around the metal. He hoped Seth remembered he couldn't stand long like this, but as he watched Seth soap the sponge, all concerns other than getting Seth's hands on his skin flew out of his head.

Seth took his time caressing James's body with the suds, running it along the planes of his chest and abs, down his arms and legs. He shivered hard when Seth used the suds to cover his engorged and weeping cock, stroking it only a few times before the hand slipped between his legs to tease his opening, putting him on edge so fast it took his breath away.

He moaned and shifted to widen his stance but made sure not to let go of the showerhead; he feared Seth would stop if he did. Seth's hand left and he whimpered at the loss. Before he could object, Seth's hand returned slicked with shower gel to tease James's rim before slowly pushing inside. Seth took his time cleaning and preparing James, and by the time he stopped, James was mewling and trembling so hard he could barely hold on.

"Please sir, I—I need…." He was so hard and he felt so empty. He needed Seth to fill him, to surround him, to take him.

Seth quickly rinsed James off and grabbed a large bath sheet to dry James and then himself. Even the brush of the towel was torture on his oversensitized skin. Once dry and out of the shower, Seth lifted James into his arms. James wrapped his legs around Seth's waist, his arms around his neck. He leaned in and nuzzled his cheek.

He kissed his way to Seth's ear as Seth carried James to their bed. "I need you in me, sir. Please." He knew he was begging but he didn't care. He was dying to have Seth buried in his body, pleasing them both. He shifted his hips to grind into Seth's but was cut short when he found himself bounced on the bed.

"Middle of the bed, pet. Now." He turned and padded into the closet.

James shifted to the center on his back, bent his knees and tilted his pelvis to make sure his cock and hole were displayed, hoping to hurry Seth along with whatever he had planned. Watching Seth intently, one of James's hands strayed to his abdomen, stroking the skin before it slid to a taught nipple.

"Hands above your head, those are for me to play with, not you. Your body is mine when we're in bed." The powerful commanding tone of his words sent a thrill through James's body, and he obediently raised his hands above his head. They had done this before, and Seth had never hurt him or pushed him too far.

James watched, eager and aching, as Seth approached. He noticed that Seth had a few pieces of cloth in his hands but didn't think anything of it until he spoke.

"James." Seth waited until he met his gaze. "I would like to play a little more tonight. You were fine with the scarves before, will you trust me again?"

"That's more than a scarf, isn't it?" James stared at Seth's items, nervous yet curious. He had been doing a little research on what submission was, but most of what he found included pain or humiliation—neither was appealing or tolerable to him. Seth wouldn't hurt him, though, he was sure of it.

"It is. One is a blindfold, your scarf for holding, of course, and a ribbon. The last item is for a little sensation play. You will like it, I assure you, pet."

James looked into Seth's ever-changing hazel eyes and saw nothing but desire and love. He knew it would be okay. He nodded. "I trust you, sir."

Seth climbed onto the bed and kissed James, slanting his mouth over James's in a demanding show of passion. James could do nothing but open his mouth and accept Seth's tongue as it possessed him so completely that only Seth existed. After a moment, he joined in, licking his tongue across Seth's, arching his body up to meet its other half.

Just as suddenly as it started, the kiss stopped. Seth pulled back, and for the first time, James noticed his wrists were already wrapped with the scarf, the cloth draped across the palms of his hands. *Damn he's good at that!*

"Just like before, if you need me to stop, let go of the scarf. I am not going to tie down your wrists." James nodded, not able to speak as his body trembled. "Good."

James watched as Seth picked up the long piece of ribbon. It was a deep indigo, and by the sheen, he thought it might be satin, or meant to look like it. It startled him to also note there was a small pair of scissors in the pile. "What are those for?" he asked and nodded to the ribbon and scissors.

"Trust, pet, means I am in control and you willingly accept what I deem is needed for our mutual enjoyment."

That wasn't an answer as far as James was concerned, but he closed his eyes and reminded himself that he trusted Seth and wanted to please his lover as much as, if not more so than, he wanted to be pleased. He took a deep breath, let it out slowly, then opened his eyes to watch Seth's strong hands wrap the ribbon around one wrist and tie it carefully before snipping off the excess. He did the same to the other wrist and then trailed his fingers down James's arms in a featherlight caress.

Seth slid his hands back to James's wrists and traced the ribbon, the dark indigo a startling contrast against James's pale skin. "Not too tight?"

"No, sir."

"Good. Lift your head, please."

James did as ordered. Seth quickly slid the remainder of the ribbon around James's throat and knotted it, leaving a long tail, which he trailed down James's chest.

Seth's hand slid around his neck and convulsed at the nape as he let out a deep growl. James could see the flash of heat and lust in his eyes. "I knew that color would look delicious against your skin."

Before the flutter in his gut could distract him, he asked, "Why?"

"Why the ribbons, baby?" Seth skimmed his hands over his shoulders.

James nodded when words failed him, Seth's hands keeping his body wound so tight he had trouble thinking.

"You are not ready for true bindings of any kind, but I want to see how you will look one day, all stretched out for me, wearing nothing but the tokens I give you," Seth explained, his swirling hazel eyes deep with barely restrained passion and longing.

James let out a moan at the thought of being possessed in such a manner by his lover.

Seth's hands had not stopped teasing and exploring the entire time, and he now bent to his task, kissing his way down and then back up to James's small, tight nipples. Drawing the hardened bud into his mouth, he flicked it with his tongue before lightly biting down.

Seth's lips and teeth latched onto his throat, worrying the flesh. He felt a tug on the ribbon around his neck, but unlike the panic he expected, it made him feel possessed and desired. Seth increased the intensity of the kisses as he settled his weight onto him. James moaned and rocked his hips up into Seth, wordlessly pleading with his lover to please hurry.

Seth chuckled, the sensual tone shooting straight to James's cock. "Not yet, pet. We have a long way to go."

James wanted to cry, or possibly pounce on Seth, but was distracted from his plotting when Seth reached over and lifted a wide black scarf. "I am going to cover your eyes now, and then we will begin."

James swallowed hard but nodded. He closed his eyes before the scarf actually touched him, hoping to hide his unease from Seth.

James felt Seth's fingers card through his hair and then the scarf settle across his eyes, what little light bled through his lids suddenly absent. His breath caught and he tensed, unable to hide his fear.

"Let me ask you something, James. What are you afraid of?"

"I—"

"Are you afraid I will beat you?" James felt the tip of one of Seth's fingers slide up the underside of his cock, tracing the large vein.

James moaned and shook his head. "No!"

"Worried I will cut or pierce your skin?" The finger disappeared but returned with friends. Seth ran both hands up and down James's thighs before he pushed his legs up and out a little more, exposing his tight opening even more.

James managed to grind out a *no* as Seth worked a slicked finger around and then into his body. He hadn't even heard the snick of the lube being opened. He wrapped his hands with the scarf to hold on better and rocked against the invading finger.

"Then be a good boy, and let me love you," Seth cooed. The finger gone, James tried to reach out but the scarf kept him in place.

Something, fur maybe, gently touched his cheek before it slid down his throat and chest to tease over each nipple in turn. It was an odd sensation, the silky slide of the fur against his hot skin. Seth continued to stroke his chest and thighs with the material, sometimes with a touch so light it tickled. Unable to see, he had no way of predicting where the fur would touch next, which served to heighten every touch, sound, and feeling.

After an eternity, or so it seemed to James, of the sensual teasing, the fur wrapped around his cock in a solid grip. "*Oh God....*" The fur wrapped fist began to stroke in long, slow pulls, drawing out a groan that James was sure came straight from his soul. The sensation was strange, a silky slide and then prickles as the hand slid in the other direction. The other hand reached out to pinch and roll his nipples, effectively overloading his body in sensation.

"Don't tense up and do *not* come yet." All touch suddenly stopped. Seth remained settled between his thighs, but for the longest time there was no touch or sound other than their breathing, until the telltale rip of foil and Seth shifting. *Oh God, please let this be it. Please....*

With no other warning, Seth pressed into his entrance. James fought to breathe as Seth continued to push in, not stopping until he was fully seated. James moved to meet Seth's unrelenting passion, tossing his head back and forth in ecstasy. The sensations were so powerful, he knew he wouldn't last, not with all the sensual torture Seth had already put him through. He just hoped Seth wouldn't deny him his release for much longer.

"I can't, sir. Please let me come!" James barely managed to keep himself from screaming as he begged.

Seth hitched James's legs higher, slamming into him over and over. The ribbon around his neck pulled sharply against his throat at Seth's command. "Now, pet. Come for me."

Painting his chest and stomach with his hot seed, James keened and shook, arching his back, which drove Seth deeper. Seth continued to pound into his body, snapping his hips harder and faster than ever. The driving slams against his prostate along with the rest of the sensations helped to prolong James's orgasm, drawing it out until his vision went white and the world stopped.

As the world righted itself and came back into focus, James wondered at the strange but wonderful floating sensation. Seth's exquisite hands caressed him, which helped him focus more, but his whole being felt the bliss of being wrapped in Seth's arms and soul.

It was in that state that James drifted off to sleep, happy in Seth's arms.

chapter nineteen

AS JAMES woke up, what he saw, both with his eyes closed and open, was what called him to his studio before the sun began to lighten the sky. By the time he realized he was being watched, he had already been up for hours.

"Mother," Seth whispered behind him. "He hates when people watch him paint. He never lets others see his work until he is satisfied with whatever he is working on."

"But look at him paint, dear, how can you not watch him?"

"Agreed, but…."

James tried to push away their whispered conversation but to no avail. Thankfully he was about done with his newest and final piece for the show. Britt would be by later that week to pick her pieces for the event. He hoped she would be happy with his offerings to her gallery.

"Do you think he will sell me the one he's working on now, Seth?" James could hear Terra's lilting voice. Her accent was beautiful. He idly wondered why Seth's wasn't the same. Once in a while, when he was really turned on or exhausted, a little of the same brogue his parents spoke in would surface, but it was rare.

He put down the brush he had been using, and turned in his art chair to face them. "Terra, this one is for the gallery show next weekend. I can't sell it, but, um… if you would like you can join us at the show. The theme is touch and there will be many other artists shown as well."

"Stop abusing your lip, baby," Seth chided gently. James released his bottom lip. He hadn't realized he had been biting it until then. "I already acquired passes for them to join us. Are you done for now?"

"Yes. I need to clean up, though." He paused to look quickly at Terra and then back to Seth. "Did I forget something?"

"Yes, baby. They invited us to brunch last night. So, go get your shower and I will lock up your studio for you." Seth swatted his butt on his way past. He could hear Terra's soft giggle as he closed the door to the bedroom, leaving them all behind.

SETH'S car service picked them up and drove them to an exclusive club for brunch—Rhys followed close on his bike. The elegance of the building was intimidating, but James put on his best smile and he and Seth followed Seth's parents inside. He was certain he looked like the poor cousin compared to Seth and his parents. Even Rhys had dressed up, though he was quiet and in the background as he guarded, not trusting the club security after the latest threat. James was silently glad, though he wasn't about to voice that relief.

The inside was even more beautiful, surprising James. An elf-like woman glided to them and after speaking with Scott, led them to a partially secluded table. Once everyone was seated, the hostess passed out menus and left, letting them know their server would be right out. Only a moment or so later, people descended on the group, filling glasses, offering wine and starters—busy but subdued at the same time.

Seth ordered for James and himself. James noticed Scott nod to himself, a pleased, small smile on his lips. *Guess he really did learn most of his behaviors, outside the bedroom, from his parents. Cool.*

"So," Terra began as she leaned in and patted his hand. "Are you excited about the show?"

"I think terrified would be a better word. Your son convinced me, with help from my best friend, Chase, to cut back my hours at work and focus more on my art." He still worried that Seth was making a much bigger deal about his art than he should and worried that he would not be able to afford the cut in hours. But Seth and Brittany had assured him his work was good enough, and Carl, his boss at Skye Designs, had promised he still had his job.

"I *have* seen your work, dear boy. It's very good. With him and Brittany behind you, you have nothing to fear."

James smiled, charmed by her faith in him and her loyalty and certainty in Seth. But then, the fastest way to win James over was to make Seth and Danni happy. "Thank you, ma'am."

"I told you, it's Terra. No need for formality." She patted his hand again.

Brunch was pleasant and things seemed to be going well until near the end. Rhys's cell rang, and when he answered, his face went from stoic to furious.

James watched as Rhys and Seth stepped away from the table, whispering furiously. After a few minutes they both came back to the table. "Mother, Father, I hate to do this but James and I have to go. Now." He bit out the last word.

Rhys was beside James with his forearm crutches in hand. "Here. We need to get back to your house before the cops do. Hurry."

Before long they were rushing to the cottage, James trying desperately not to panic. "What's going on, Seth? Why did we just run out of there?"

"Someone tried to set our home on fire. Well, your studio at least. Mark caught them but not before the fire was set."

"My house? My art? Oh, God!" James trembled so hard he was grateful Seth had waited to tell him until after they left *and* he was sitting. He was pretty sure Seth said more but he heard none of it. All he could think about was his art and his home. Someone hated him enough to attack his home? What had he ever done to deserve such violence?

The fire department and police were already there when they arrived, much to his relief. James couldn't understand why the arsonist/stalker wanted to hurt him, but the thought of dealing with this without the police there was not a pleasant idea either.

His lawn was covered in firemen, hoses, and cops and the flashing lights hurt his eyes, but he was thankful for all of them. Dal, though he was in his police uniform, was the first official responder to come over to them. Seth held him tightly, he figured to stop him from bolting into the house to find out what damage was done.

"James?"

"Huh?" James mumbled, his focus entirely on the smoke coming from the back of his home. "What?"

"James, Mr. Bryant." That caught his attention, partially. "The fire didn't get inside. It's ok."

"It didn't?" James asked. Dal had his attention completely.

"No, sir. The person Mark caught tried to set your stone cottage on fire with, basically, Molotov cocktails. Had this been a wood home, it would have caused a lot of damage, I bet, but to stone? Just some charring probably."

James sagged in Seth's arms. "So, you caught the stalker?" Seth asked, holding James tightly.

"Yes, sir. But um, I don't know if he was the one behind the threats and attack or if he's just one of many."

Dal shuffled his feet back and forth. "What aren't you telling me, Dal?"

"It's sick, man! How can you defend perverts like them?" someone screamed on the other side of the yard.

James's head snapped up, and he stared as the voice continued to spew forth hate and disgust. He recognized that voice. *Oh, God, it can't be. No, no, no!*

"Someone get him in the car, now!" Dal snapped.

Before anyone knew what was happening, the screaming man broke free and charged at James and Seth, though James figured it was really just at him—Seth was just in the wrong place. Without thought, James pushed Seth hard, causing him to stumble and fall to the side just as he braced for Joey, James's linebacker-sized baby brother, to slam into him.

It took a moment to realize that Rhys and Dal intercepted Joey and that Dal was in the process of pulling him up out of the dirt.

Before he could get himself together enough to say anything, Seth was back by his side, holding him tight. After a few moments, he realized Seth was more holding him up than holding on to him. *My own brother tried to set my house on fire?* James could not make sense of the events.

Dal drug Joey off and shoved him into the back of his police car. As he moved away, he snapped at someone James didn't know, "Why wasn't he in the damn car already?" The venom in the second set of instructions chilled James to the core.

Everything after that was a blur.

HIS mother had called him for the first time in years, demanding that he come down to the station and "fix" it—like it was his fault Joey and Mike were in jail. James was unsure what to expect, but feared the confrontation just the same. At the last moment he decided against asking Seth to take off work to accompany him, both because he didn't want to subject Seth to his mother's vitriol and because he knew he needed to face her himself, no matter how much he did *not* want to.

James knew they had to be an interesting sight—he and his entourage—as they entered the police station to deal with his family and their problems. Chase walked beside him, to his left, with Mel Holcomb, his lawyer, to his right, and Rhys in front. He didn't see why Rhys needed to act as his guard anymore, but he had been out-voted and told to "suck it up." He'd thought of a few things he would have liked to suck, but only on Seth.

"Mr. Bryant," called a deep voice, one James did not know. The man before him was shorter than him, about five-nine or so, heavyset with dark curly hair cut in a high-n-tight. He stood next to

Officer Dal Sayer, who was in his uniform. "I'm Detective Carthage. You already know Officer Sayer. Thank you for coming down."

James nodded and took the hand the detective extended.

"Hello, sir. This is Mr. Holcomb, my attorney, Chase Manning my best friend and assistant, and Rhys Sayer, my bodyguard," James explained as he gestured to each man in turn.

"I understand that it was actually Mrs. Bryant, James's mother, who requested this meeting, is that correct?" Mel asked. He had already instructed James to let him handle most of the talking, something he was more than happy to cooperate with. The thought of seeing his mother again terrified him.

"Yes, she is insisting that this is not a criminal issue, but rather a sibling problem and that you will drop the charges against Joseph Bryant," Carthage explained, looking past Mel, to James. "She is also very vocal about Officer Mike Delanco's arrest. But, as I already explained to your mother, Mr. Bryant, you cannot not drop the charges, that it was out of your hands due to hate crimes and arson. However, considering your family history, and the nature of the situation we chose to sponsor the meeting here at the police department for your safety."

"I bet she is," Chase grumbled. He slid his right hand down James's back, settling it on his lower back. "James, you don't have to do this. Mel can deal with all the legal stuff, ya know."

"Yes," James murmured. He opened his mouth to continue when he heard a voice he thought to never hear again. His mother barreled toward him, face streaked with tears and skin blotchy from crying.

"James!" James stared at her as she raced forward. For the longest time, James had hoped to have a chance to talk with his mother again, but not like this…. Not where she was again siding with someone who hurt him. For a moment James wondered why she couldn't love him too, but he knew that was a line of thought that led nowhere good.

Rhys and Chase stepped in front of James at the same time—
James would find it amusing later, when he had a chance to think
back on the day—effectively blocking access to her oldest child.

"Move out of my way, now! I need to speak to James. I won't
have my son locked up like some common criminal!"

"Ma'am," Rhys rumbled. He folded his massive arms across
his chest as he stared her down. "Your younger son stalked and
terrorized James and his family. He then attempted to set his home
on fire. These are the facts of the situation. Now, take a step back."

James watched as Chase took almost the same stance, though
he was so much smaller than Rhys. "Is there somewhere this farce of
a meeting can move to so Jamie can sit down?" Chase snapped.

James wasn't sure whom he was asking, but Dal came to the
rescue. "I have a room ready. This way, please." Once everyone
filed in, Detective Carthage pushed the door closed.

Mel and James sat on one side of the conference table, while
Chase and Rhys continued to stand, flanking them. Dianne, James's
mother, sat primly across from him and glowered between James
and Chase. Dal and Carthage kept neutral positions on the side.

"You will drop these ridiculous charges against Joey, this
instant! He's a good boy, a good son, and I will not have you
destroy his life with your perversions. I want the charges against
Mike dropped as well. He's a good cop."

He stared at his mother, debating how to respond to her insane
demands and assertions. Joey and Mike good boys? Hearing her side
with them, again, made his stomach hurt and his head spin. "You
never listened when I was a kid and told you what they did to me,
well now you have no choice but to deal with it. Joey is not a good
boy and Mike?" He gave a sad, humorless laugh. "He's nothing
more than a bully and rapist who gets off on hurting others."

James couldn't continue to speak as his mother screeched
about how he was going to hell and that she would not allow his
depravities to destroy her family. Hearing her shunted James back to
being that scared teen who wanted nothing more than for his parents
to love him enough to protect him.

"That's enough!" Dal Sayer boomed. "Your *son* is the victim of a hate crime, stalking, and arson. Unless you want charges leveled at you as well, I would suggest you tone it down and treat Mr. Bryant with some respect. Making threats in front of a lawyer and the police?" He shook his head but stopped speaking.

"Hates me," James mumbled. He wasn't sure when he had started to speak, but it only came out as a whisper. "Why can't she love me too...?"

"James?" He felt Chase's hand on his cheek. "Don't go there, hun. You have a family, a real one. Seth, Danni, me. She doesn't matter." Chase shifted and wrapped his arms around James from behind.

"There is no point in continuing this meeting," Mel stated. "Mr. Bryant will not be dropping the charges against Joseph Bryant. He has nothing to do with the arson charge or the charges against Michael Delanco, that's all internal. If you continue to harass or threaten James or his family, I will file a restraining and gag order against you."

"Family? You mean that sodomite he lives with? They live with a small child! Did you know that? How can you sit there and allow what goes on in that house, to that little child!"

"Enough! Chase, take James home," Rhys growled as he cut her ranting off.

"No," James whispered. He cleared his throat and tried again. "No. I have something I need to say first." James's eyes swept over his friends before he squared his shoulders and faced his mother. "I've spent the last twelve or so years trying to figure out how to make you love me like a mother is supposed to, but I can see that you would rather praise the boys that abused me, violated my home, and nearly destroyed me, than open your eyes or heart to your own flesh and blood, so fine! Go cry for Joey. Go pine for Mike." His fingers ached from how hard he clutched the grips of his forearm crutches, but he managed to stand his ground, though he wasn't sure how. "But stay the hell out of my life and away from my real family. If you ever so much as look at Seth or Danni you will regret it! You are dead to me, as is Father! Never again, you hear me?" James knew he was shaking. He stared down at the woman who had been his mother as she gaped at him.

Chase moved to get James walking but stopped at the door, looking back at the monster that inhabited the body of the woman James remembered making him soup and kissing his boo-boos when he was little. James paused when he heard Chase speak. "James's home is warm, loving, protective, and caring. All the things a home should be. Instead of tearing him down, you should be proud of the man he has become. Successful artist, doting stepfather, loyal friend and brother. I don't know how he turned out as well as he did with people like you in his life, but do us all a favor and stay away from him!"

He was crying when Chase looked at him again. Hearing how Chase felt about him made him realize he truly did have a family. One he would fight to keep.

chapter twenty

JAMES and Chase returned to the house that evening to find Seth home. Seth had called earlier and told him he had a couple more appointments and for him not to rush home. He said he would provide dinner. Danni was at dance for another hour—they had put her in dance class and she loved it.

Chase followed him when he entered the house and they both froze. Sitting on his couch was a young woman speaking animatedly with Seth. After the day he just finished, a stranger in his home was not high on his list of happy thoughts.

The woman barely looked legal. She perked up when she saw him and Chase standing there staring. "Oh, this must be your partner, James." She popped up to her feet and, graceful as a dancer, came over and extended her hand to James. "Hello, sir."

James took her offered hand on autopilot but looked to Seth for an explanation.

"James, this is Sydney Green. If you like her too, I plan to hire her as our housekeeper and nanny." His words took James aback for a moment, but they had discussed hiring someone to help around the house after Terra brought it up, and with Danni, instead of having the cleaning service he had always used.

James turned back to the hopeful looking woman. "Hello, Sydney."

"Hi. I will be serving dinner soon. Is your friend staying?"

Her perky attitude and youth worried James, but he trusted Seth to do what was right. "Chase? Are you staying?"

"Thanks but no. I have a date but Seth, man.... A housekeeper?"

Seth's face split in a huge smile, relaxing James immediately. "She was a friend of Quinn's who used to babysit Danni once in a while. She will help keep the place clean, cook only when James is too tired or does not wish to, and even help with homework. It will help James out and me by extension. Now I don't have to worry about James trying to do too much." Seth's eyes bored into James's. "And she just finished a couple of culinary classes along with her early childhood care and education courses. You two should have a ball in the kitchen."

The satisfied look on Seth's face had James willing to agree to almost anything. "Okay, sir. But," he continued, looking back at Sydney, "I like cooking for my family and my studio is off limits. Not even Seth goes in without me." That was the one place he ruled, and housekeeper or not, no one was allowed near his paints and work.

"Yes, sir. Seth explained. I will only cook if you need me to and I don't blame you about your studio. I'm the same way about my jewelry making."

James smiled, pleased with her easy acceptance of his one real rule. "Thank you. Um, I don't mean to be rude, but does that mean you're moving in?"

Sydney shook her head. "I already have a home with my husband."

After a few more pleasantries, she headed for the kitchen and Chase left to get ready for his date. Seth pulled him into his arms, a gentle, soothing caress up and down his back. "You know why I want this for you, baby?"

"Yes, sir. You worry that I do too much."

"Yes, baby. Plus, she will help in the evenings with Danni. Now, come here. What did you find out?"

James groaned. He *so* didn't want to discuss what had happened at the police station. "You know my mother requested I come down there after not having spoken to me in nearly a decade?"

"Yes, baby. Now, what happened? You look strange but in much better spirits than I expected given where you were."

"She demanded I drop the charges against Joey, which I did *not* do," he added. "She also tried to blame me for his arrest, and for Mike's. They are charging him with... I don't remember what, but something for his helping Joey do this to us."

"You dealt with your mother? You seem good, considering...."

"I am. Chase reminded me of something while we were there. I have a family, and my parents and Joey are not part of it. Family doesn't turn its back on you. You are part of my family and my future, not her."

"What about your father?"

"It was only her. With how she was, I assume it was a good thing that he stayed away, though I was surprised. Maybe he was in with Joey?"

James shrugged and tried to change the direction of their evening. He leaned in to Seth, breathing in his unique scent as he nuzzled his jaw. "Thank you for—for everything, sir."

Seth turned his face to meet James's, taking his lips in a soft, exploring kiss.

JAMES took every opportunity that evening to touch, tease, and entice Seth. He felt disconnected and adrift in his relationship with Seth lately and needed his lover, even with his revelation earlier. By the time they entered their bedroom, James trembled in anticipation of what Seth might do to him.

"Do you know what you need, baby?" Seth asked, pinning him in place with those piercing hazel eyes.

"You," he panted. "To please you." His cock was so hard. He could barely breathe waiting to hear what Seth would say. James needed him on such a deep level that he could barely think.

"You do that, baby, just by existing." Seth leaned in, guiding James down and onto the bed.

James whimpered when Seth took his mouth roughly, delving inside, nibbling on his lips, and simply overwhelming James into dazed bliss.

"You want me to fuck your face, pet?" Seth asked when he finally tore his mouth away, watching James gasp for air. "Control your body, your pleasure, your very breath? You'd like that, wouldn't you, baby?"

Oh, God! James stopped breathing as the idea worked its way through his mind and into his cock. He whimpered with need, knowing with Seth it was mutual passion and his needs and wants were cared about. That *he* was cared about.

"Move for me, pet," Seth murmured, gently guiding James so that he was on his back and his head was hanging partway off the bed.

"I'm going to fill that pretty mouth of yours, baby. I'm going to take you until I decide to stop and you are going to stay right there, knowing it's my pleasure you serve, our pleasure. You will not come unless I give you permission. Do you understand?" Seth asked as he stroked James's cock a few times.

Seth's voice and touch were the same, gentle but firm, and it made James want to submit, to give over everything and simply feel. His body trembled as his mind registered the truth of his thoughts. He wanted Seth to take control, needed it. James licked his plump, kiss-swollen lips and nodded.

"I need to hear it, baby. Are you ready?"

He nodded as he moaned, "Please, sir. Please let me please you."

Seth stroked his hair and bent to kiss him possessively. "Such a good boy."

Seth stood, reached over to the side table, and removed two lengths of smooth indigo ribbon. "Sit up for a moment." As he began to wrap and bind James's arms to his sides, Seth explained calmly, "I don't want to hurt you, so you have to tell me immediately if the ribbon becomes too much. I will be very displeased if you allow yourself to be injured, pet."

When he couldn't move his hands or arms, Seth seemed pleased. He gently stroked James a few times, chuckling when his plaintive cries slipped out as he stretched his head toward Seth's delicious cock.

Having mercy on him, Seth lowered himself and pressed against his lips. Instinctively James opened his mouth, inhaling Seth's slightly spicy, musky scent. The strength of his reaction shocked him when his body shuddered, and damn near orgasmed just from the scent and feel of Seth's silky crown sliding between his lips.

Using his tongue and lips, he stroked and sucked Seth, using a subtle twist of his head to enhance the movements as he whimpered and hollowed out his cheeks. He wanted to touch, but the silky ribbon stopped him, though he knew he could stop everything if he needed to. It was really more the illusion of control, but James loved that Seth cared enough to make sure they both felt safe and loved while together.

After a time Seth thrust carefully, sliding between his lips. The thrusts became deeper and finally he felt Seth's cock cut off his air. Seth held still for a moment and then backed off, returning to his thrusting. Cutting off his air and how long he held like that slowly increased until James writhed as he desperately sucked his lover closer to orgasm.

With one more thrust, Seth slid to the back of his throat as he came. James did his best to swallow again and again, taking everything Seth gave him. Just as the lack of air was making his head swim, James felt Seth's lips wrap around his member and suck hard. Seth softened, though very slowly.

His body started to thrust up of its own accord. He worried that he wouldn't be able to hold off much longer when Seth popped off long enough to command, "Now, pet. I want every drop!"

His mouth clamped around James again and he felt his orgasm slam into him. It started, he was certain, in his soul and spread throughout his body. Shockwave after wave of pleasure rocked his body and mind until all that existed was Seth.

His mind floated as Seth withdrew, cleaned him, and released the ribbons, perfectly content and satisfied. No one had ever loved him like Seth. No one had ever given him such pleasure, either. He didn't know what he'd done to gain Seth's love and attention, but he vowed to himself to do everything in his power to keep Seth for the rest of their lives.

SETH entered their bedroom and looked around. He had laid out James's clothes; now he simply had to corral his wayward lover into them in time to make the opening of the *Touch* show at the gallery. He also fought to keep his nerves hidden. He had things to do tonight, and sending James into a panic attack early would not help either of them.

Lost in thought, he missed the bathroom door opening and James's entrance. He was wearing only a towel around his waist as he maneuvered on his crutches over to the bed.

Seth took in the long line of his lover, his partner in life, love, and home, suppressing a groan when James unceremoniously dropped the towel.

James looked back over his shoulder and smirked. "You even laid out my best sticks, I see."

Seth shrugged. "And?"

"Thank you, love." The smirk shifted into a beatific smile. Seth's main goal in life was to continue to put that smile on his James's face. Well, and put a similar one on his little princess's face.

Sydney, the new housekeeper, had taken Danni out with her, so there would be no delays in their departure to the gallery. She would be tucked in and asleep long before they were to return that evening.

"Now, get dressed. The car will be here soon and you cannot go to the show like that," he added, gesturing to the lack of clothing on James's body.

"Give me ten minutes and I will be out front." James continued to smile, but Seth could see how he struggled not to fidget. He knew James was nervous but was impressed with how well he hid it. Most people would never notice.

"Get ready, then," Seth said before turning and heading to the main room.

While he waited, he fidgeted. The small box hidden in his tux was burning a hole in his pocket, and he thought over the possible responses James might give.

The *tick-step* of James entering the room drew his attention. When he turned to look, a groan slipped out. God, his man in a tux was amazing. The charcoal gray Armani tuxedo with indigo vest and Euro tie looked delicious. He couldn't wait to get James home again later and out of it.

James accompanied Seth to the door as the doorbell rang. Chase and Scott, Seth's dad, greeted them in their own tuxes. Scott was cool confidence, while Chase looked like he might come apart any second with excitement. "Ready?" Chase asked.

Together the four men headed toward the long black limousine parked in front of James's stone cottage. Seth helped James inside before joining the others. Soft music played, and Seth's mother, Terra, perched primly on one plush seat.

Conversation was light as Seth and James were nervous, although for very different reasons. Seth was wholly confident in the success of James's work in the show, unlike James. Seth was more worried about afterward. The ride wasn't long, and before they knew it they pulled up in front of Britt's gallery.

James froze as he stared at the building. Seth noticed before the others. He slid his hand down James's back and leaned in. "You deserve this, baby. Now smile and go with Chase while I get my parents settled inside. I will meet you right inside the doors."

James audibly swallowed and nodded before leaning into Seth.

"Chase?" Seth whispered.

"On it. You stay with James and I'll get your parents settled inside."

Seth smiled and held his nervous partner, rubbing circles on his back until he pulled himself together.

Inside they all met up again, and after the formal opening, the group was met by Rhys and Dal Sayer.

"Thank you for inviting us," Dal said. He and Rhys were decked out in well-cut suits.

"Well, Rhys is one of my subjects so it only seemed fair." James became friends with both men while the stalking and threats had been happening. He was glad to see that both men seemed to think the same about James. The tension between Chase and Rhys was still a problem, though thankfully James did not seem to care, being friends with both.

Rhys leaned in and whispered, "Everything is all set, Seth. You sure you want to do it here?"

"Here is the perfect place and I already talked to Danni so relax."

Rhys nodded as he backed away.

"This is amazing," Scott commented as they began to wander through the art collections.

"James's work is wonderful. The first print I sent you was the finished work of the sketch he was working on the first time he came to my office. I only wish he could see his work the way others do." Seth sighed as he thought about the scene when Brittany had stopped by to collect the pieces for the show. She had picked more than James expected, including two he had shelved, having been unhappy with how they turned out. She won, of course.

"Your mother told me the story around that painting and your dinner afterward." They both chuckled as Seth turned to take in his lover as he stood to the side and answered questions from various patrons and critics.

"Seth?" Terra tapped him on his arm.

"Yes, Mother?"

"Why do some of the works have little colored tags beside the nameplates?"

"Those are reserved or sold already. All the works displayed are for sale but Britt's not going to take down work while the show is still on. This lets buyers know which are still available. As you may notice, almost all of James's already have dots even though we have only been here a short time."

"Yes," Terra replied, her voice drawn. It seemed to match the wistful look in her eyes. "Someone already purchased the one I wanted the most."

Seth saw his father wink at him from behind his mother's back. Neither James nor Terra knew Scott had arranged for its purchase and shipping before the show. He would allow his father to decide when to reveal his gift for her.

Seth and James wandered around the gallery after the group split up to look around. James worked so hard, not allowing even the stalking and attack to distract him from finishing everything for the show. Seth still couldn't believe it had been James's brother who threatened them. He had been certain that Chase was right, that it was Danni's grandparents, but the attack had been the worst. It also set in motion what Seth was about to do.

As they rounded a corner, Seth led James to an area that had been decked out with flowers, soft lighting, and a plush bench. James sat and waited for Seth to settle beside him. After a moment, Seth took his left hand into his own.

"I know that touch is the theme of tonight's show but it's not the art on the wall that is the true treasure. When we first met, you intrigued me, and then that first brush of a kiss after dinner a week later stole my breath and heart. You were so beautiful and fragile yet you were also so, so strong."

He watched as various emotions flitted over James's face before he continued.

"I knew from that moment on that I wanted you in my life. I wanted someone that I could love and would love me too in return. The trust you have offered me I will cherish just as I do you. Always."

Seth slid off the bench and settled on one knee in front of James. Reaching into his pocket, he retrieved a small velvet and silk box he had fidgeted with all evening.

"Seth," James exhaled, his eyes so big and wet Seth rushed to finish before James panicked or cried.

"I know I said I would not ask you to marry me if it meant that you would ever be left to wonder if I meant it, but I hope you know by now how much I love and cherish you, baby." Seth watched as James nodded, a single tear leaking from the edge of one eye.

"Would you make Danni and me the happiest people ever by becoming our family forever?"

"Are you sure, Seth?" James whispered. James's hand trembled in his as he continued to hold him.

"A bonding between personalities, between souls that are so perfect they may as well have been made for the other, and together they make a perfect balance of power, passion, and love. To some, on the outside, the power might seem unbalanced, but to the souls in question, it is perfect. A perfection so beautiful that the gods themselves weep for the harmony of the union. That is what I see when I look at you. What I want with you. I have never been surer of anything, James. You are my future. Marry me?"

James stared at him for an eternity, or so it seemed to Seth, and he swallowed hard a couple of times. It took him three tries to reply. "Yes, Seth. Please, yes!"

Seth surged forward and wrapped his arms around James, holding on for dear life, and he felt James do the same to him. From behind them, Seth heard applause. When James lifted his head off Seth's shoulder, they turned their heads to look at the gathered crowd. Seth noted that those closest to them—even Mel and Britt had snuck in—were all beaming.

"You need to actually put the ring on the man, ya know," Chase quipped.

Seth felt his face get hot but simply turned back to James and slipped the platinum and sapphire band onto his finger.

"Always," he whispered as the show and crowd surged back to life around them.

TEMPESTE O'RILEY is an out and proud omnisexual/bi woman whose best friend growing up had the courage to do what she couldn't—defy the hate and come out. He has been her hero ever since.

Tempe is a hopeless romantic who loves strong relationships and happily-ever-afters. Though new to writing M/M, she has done many things in her life, yet writing has always drawn her back—no matter what else life has thrown her way. She counts her friends, family, and Muse as her greatest blessings in life. She lives in Wisconsin with her children, reading, writing, and enjoying life.

Tempe is also a proud member of Romance Writers of America® and Rainbow Romance Writers.

Learn more about Tempeste and her writing
at http://tempesteoriley.com or
https://www.facebook.com/TempesteORiley.author.

A STEEL CITY STORY

WILD
HORSES

KATE PAVELLE

Leather + Lace

A.B. GAYLE